RAISING WOMEN

PRAISE FOR RAISING WOMEN

"Raising Women is a book that knows you. It knows all your secrets. It knows all the thoughts you've had. It knows what choices you've made, as well as the choices you'd change if you could go back and be a teenage girl again. It also knows that sometimes, a little self-discovery is the scariest thing of all."
– Rebecca Jones-Howe, author of *Vile Men* and *Ending in Ashes*

"Less a journey and more a plummet through a mad funhouse of personal discovery, risky behaviors, and strange bedfellows, to a place where the reader overturns narrative stones and returns time and again for those left unturned, and the questionable choices become their own with every turn of the page."
– Jason M. Fylan, author of "Engines, O-Rings, and Astronauts" in *Burnt Tongues*

"Raising Women offers insight on how to acknowledge the human being and their experience, shattering any judgements of what a "real" woman should be, look and think like."
– Lianna Albrizio, *Reedsy Discovery*

"Waite builds a story with consistencies through each path."
– Courtnee Turner Hoyle, *Readers' Favorite* ★★★★★

RAISING WOMEN

an interactive novel

SHANNON WAITE

Shannon Waite
Detroit, Michigan

ISBN: 979-8-9910164-0-7 (print)
ISBN: 979-8-9910164-1-4 (e-book)

Library of Congress Control Number: 2024916452

Cover images by Lindee Robinson Photography
Cover art and interior formatting by Qamber Designs

First edition

Visit the author's website at www.shannonwaiteauthor.com

DIRECTIONS

Do not read *Raising Women* from beginning to end. Instead, you will find that from time to time you'll be asked to make a choice. This is because the story is powered by your decisions.

As a result, you will experience challenges that a host of irresponsible characters present to you as a sixteen-year-old girl in the Midwest. When you make a decision, follow the instructions to move to the designated page to continue reading. You will know when you've arrived at an ending when you see the drawn line.

This book gives you the opportunity to read it over and over, learning new secrets about the characters and understanding how different experiences impact your story.

In this interactive novel, you have twenty-four possible pathways with four unique endings to explore the wild that is growing up girl. Good luck.

YOU AND ROMAN ARE TWO GIRLS eating donuts you grabbed from the self-serve station at the grocery store while you walk around, window shopping for things you'll never buy. Roman has pink frosting and sprinkles smeared across her bottom lip as she picks up a pair of combat boots with the hand that's not holding the donut. You stop, she looks them over, then drops them on the floor – not where she grabbed them from – and keeps going.

Sometimes you forget that Roman is actually a woman.

She's twenty-one or twenty-two. You met her at a gas station where, out of nowhere, she leaned herself against your car at the pump and asked you where you buy your hair dye. Her hair was pulled straight back. Tied with one of those twist ties that come on the plastic bread bag. You just told her you don't. "It's natural." She told you it's beautiful.

She introduced herself. She was eating Cheetos out of a bag. Had orange fingers. She licked her fingers clean and tried shaking your hand.

She asked you about your favorite band. Then she asked you what you'd sing at karaoke night. You don't sing, so you were not sure. She told you she'd sing Duran Duran's "Hungry Like the Wolf" and asked again what you'd sing. You thought of "Smells Like Teen Spirit" because Nirvana played right before you got out of your car. You wouldn't sing that though, because the real lyrics sound like misheard lyrics. They don't make sense. Then she told you you'd go out and sing that together sometime soon.

Roman's charismatic.

She told you that you'd been at the pump for a while and asked if you were done yet. You didn't know how to tell her that you finished pumping five minutes ago. Instead you asked how she got there. She laughed. Her laugh is contagious.

She got into your car.

She told you almost immediately that she'd just recently gotten out of prison. Not that long ago.

This didn't really matter to you though. Roman didn't feel threatening, even after knowing she'd been released from prison. She felt exciting.

Without you even asking, she told you that her jail time was for possession. She let her words sit for a moment, left you there on a cliffhanger and, like a joke, she finished the punchline. For possession, *and intent to distribute 500 grams or more of cocaine.*

She told you that was silly. She was never going to distribute it. That would have meant giving it all away.

But it got her thirty-six months in the slammer.

You hadn't been looking for a friend, but you never had much of a choice in the matter either (once Roman decided something, that was it). Maybe she knew something you didn't.

So now she's loitering aisles with you. This has been a frequent pastime as you get to know each other. She's always got something she needs to grab.

You place the last bite of donut in your mouth as you pass the milk aisle. Rows of whole milk, 2% fat milk, skim milk, soy milk. Roman has told you soy milk doesn't even need to be refrigerated before it's opened. It has a shelf life unopened of up to one year. You both keep walking, browsing. You pass the alcohol aisle. Pass the cleaning supplies. Pass the jewelry. It's like some sort of domestic roadshow.

You pause just a minute to stare at a diamond ring enclosed in the glass case and Roman slaps your arm.

She tells you things aren't real.

Nothing you see really exists, she says. Roman is full of advice.

You ask how. Why.

She says reality is never the same. It's always changing so how are things like rings real then if they aren't changing like reality does. She adds that reality is something we make. She picks a scab off her knuckle and lets it bleed. She's got a few more scabs up her arms.

She hasn't cut her long, dirty blonde hair for at least three years and it flutters against her cheekbones as the wind from someone walking by blows it around.

"You've got something on your lip," you say to her. She licks the frosting and thanks you.

When you first met, you asked her how long she'd been out of prison for. She told you she didn't know. Now you don't even know how long ago that was.

She did tell you, though, about how the government wants to be in your life, but not because they care about you. They just want to control you. They're like your parents. They don't give a shit, it's all about control and how they look.

Yes, of course it hurts.

She said that when they told her in prison that her time was up, she was free, there was no plan in place for where she'd go. She was just supposed to. Go, that is. Somewhere. Anywhere.

That's one of the ways people create reality, by letting the things they don't like leave their peripherals. Then it no longer exists.

To exist means to be acknowledged in some way. This is why you throw decomposing meat, moldy sourdough, and snot-dried tissues in the trash. Someone will take it somewhere else, a place you don't have to see, and then it's gone. That's how that works.

The prison pushed her out their doors and into their peripherals. They said go. She served her time.

So is she even real?

Her boobs vibrate. She digs her fist into her wife beater and pulls out a phone. It's the man who picked her up from prison calling her. He's asking where she's been.

She's not sure

She's sorry.

Maybe she knows,
But she might be wrong.

                                     She couldn't find her way back.
She will be there soon.
She promises.
        Yes, her promise means something.

        Last night was an accident.
Sorry – the last three nights were accidents.
        The phone died. She needed a charger.
        She found a charger.
                 Now it's alive.

She can come home.

Xoxo.

She pulls two suckers from the shelf closest to the exit and shoves them and her phone back in her bra.

Since you've met, she's been on and off living with a guy who told her to get in his car when prison let her free at two o'clock in the morning. She didn't really have any other option. Besides, he had a dry nose and a blood stain above his mouth. Just how she liked it.

Roman's nose has a cluster of salted freckles around it. They might be real, they might be tattoos, you don't know, but she scratches at them constantly.

She glances sideways at you and raises her thumb up to your mouth so she can wipe some sprinkles off your top lip.

You don't ask if you're going to pay for the donuts. The alarm does not buzz when you leave.

You're only sixteen.

She asks you, "Can I take you to the church I stayed at last night?" Which really means she's asking if you'll take her to the church she stayed at last night. She doesn't have a car. She can't drive, so you're the one who takes you two around.

She just got out of prison and now she needs something like a mother. You need something else.

You consider telling her yes (turn to page 7), or no – you two could just go back to your place (turn to page 13), or that you'll drop her off halfway since the halfway point is on your own way home (turn to page 17).

Roman's dad is a Presbyterian preacher.

It's not his church you're at though. He lives in some other state and Roman says all the time how grateful she is to be far far away from where she grew up with him, even if she ended up in prison over here.

At least Roman knows her dad.

The church you've pulled up to stretches tall, shadows the road it sits on, and has a dead cat – sticky, bloody fur – lying across the bottom front step. It looks like someone may have driven a steak through the creature.

Roman has told you how nowhere is ever a home, so that is definitely not what this is, but somewhere to crash when she needs it. You're not sure if they let her in or if she let herself in and never left, but she sometimes sleeps on the wooden benches next to prayer kneelers when she doesn't want to spend time with that dude she met after prison.

She leads you through three minutes of silence, the bottom of her white top rolled up, revealing a slinky belly button ring that's just two silver balls. You notice her boyfriend jeans are muddy at the bottom. You're not sure where you're going or what you're doing, but that's how it goes with Roman.

Roman knows a lot about everything. She tells you about household dust and how dead skin cells are the main ingredient. She explains how to start the engine on a VW Kessy when it has a dead battery. She explains that men will date stupid women because they're easier to control. This is why you can't ever be stupid.

The inside looks like other churches, but it's large and arched in a way that makes it feel bigger and emptier. The walls are a mud brick and the pews are red. Stained glass windows let some fake-looking light in the space, and they cage isolated angels in each one.

A woman up front is kneeling. She's the only other person in the building right now. Roman whispers to you that this is another example of the way people create reality. You nod your head.

The last time you went to church you were six and it was for your grandmother's funeral. The last time Grandmother had been to church was for her wedding. Church did not make sense. It still does not make sense.

Your mother never believed in higher powers.

Or she didn't have time for them.

Maybe both.

So she didn't pack you up, drag you through the red-rugged aisle like other children's mothers did. Instead, she sat you in front of the television and told you to pay close attention to the pictures on the screen. She must go to work. Be very good.

The expectation was that you'd be good on your own accord – not because of the threats of a Father.

Roman's told you about cemeteries under blacktops before. You researched it. It's true. They exist.

Walking through the entrance of this building feels something like walking through an old neighborhood, where everyone is a stranger.

Each step echoes.
Light-ribbons stream in front of you.
The wood smells rotten.
You watch Roman rub her fingers against her fingers.

She asks if you've ever tried wine, but before you answer, she tells you that this is a great place to get drunk for free.

From the very few times you'd attended church, you don't remember communion wine ever being enough to get someone drunk, but you trust that Roman knows what she's talking about.

She leads you past the woman who doesn't look up at you. Her hands pressed together to her chest, her eyes closed, she thinks she is watching God.

Roman walks on up the steps to the stage-looking part of the church where the pastor, priest, whoever, shouts at the people, is able to have his moment. In honor of God. During those instances, all eyes are on him. But that's what people want. Even if they say they don't. Everyone wants all eyes on them, and when it's usually only God that people pay attention to, God that everyone's begging, moments like those let people like preachers and movie stars and people performing up on stage still get to feel like God too.

Roman walks through the door that's off to the side of the church stage.

It's dark behind it.

No one calls after her.

You follow.

You stub your toe on the leg of a table and she turns around to *shh* you.

Shhh.

Just a few more steps and she leads you to the Chestnut cabinet that holds all the church wine. She gives a thumbs up, the gap in her front teeth noticeable between her split lips.

The bottles are placed together in a row. There are no glasses. This wine is normally passed out in one community goblet during church, but you imagine there must be something else to hold it in around here. Roman doesn't bother looking though. Instead, the two of you drink straight from the bottle, passing it back and forth at first, before she opens a new one as her own and leaves the rest of the first bottle to you.

You've decided wine is bitter, but you keep drinking it anyway. You don't typically drink alcohol after last time, but you promised Roman earlier that you would.

"You know in prison," Roman starts. She brings prison up a lot, so you know a lot about it even though you've never been close to going. Like, even if you one-eighty'd and killed someone tomorrow, you'd still only end up in juvie. "I was raped," she finishes.

You take another sip of wine. Almost choke on it. Stop yourself.

You're both sitting on the floor, her back arched against the corner of the wine cabinet and she rolls her head, banging it on the wood, lets a ton of wine slide down her throat like a luge.

You wonder if you're supposed to say something. Ask a question.

She picks up for you. She adds, "It's fucked up how people are sent to prison for illegal shit, but the guards who work for the prison are allowed to do illegal shit. Like shove a woman's body in the dark and lie against it like it's fabric. I told you. Everyone likes control and will play God if they have the chance." She takes a sip of wine. "Don't tell me God doesn't rape people."

You wait a second. "I'm sorry that happened to you."

She laughs in a way that sounds slurred. You're not sure how, but it is.

You know you sound stupid, but you don't know what else to say.

"You know," Roman adds, "I fucking hate cats."

Soft fur sticky with mud and blood and a wound that let the life out of it.

We all get kicked sometimes.

Sometimes it just hurts more than others.

Cats don't belong in the church anyway. There are real souls to be saved. Roman finishes off her bottle.

You ask Roman if she believes in God. You pucker your lips and put your bottle down.

If God exists, she commends him for letting Adam and Eve loose. But, she adds, people are such a mess there's no way they were made by something perfect.

The inside of the cabinet is vacant.

"Do you have any cash?" She asks you. "Let's get more wine. I mean, give me the cash and take me to the liquor store, and I'll get it." She slides a fake horizontal license out of her bra. The birthdate listed makes her six years older than she is.

You could get some more and bring it back to your house (turn to page 23), but you're not sure that's a good idea, in which case, Roman's got a different plan for you (turn to page 28).

You decide on no to the church, so you tell her she can come back to your place.

She looks ticked off, but then she agrees. But she has to grab some wine first. She'll be out in just a few. Roman goes back into the store, and you promised her you'd go back to your car to wait.

You're sitting in the '76 Jeep Cherokee your grandmother left you when she died. Your mother almost sold it. Said you were six. Said she'd get you a better car by the time you could drive, but even as a child, you knew that wouldn't be true.

Thank God she ended up keeping it. Now it's yours.

The thing is, you've only been driving it for seven months and Roman's already directed it more times than you.

You start the ignition, turn the AC and radio on. Watch a man in a trench coat walk into the store on your left. To your right, Roman pounds on the window so you'll open the locked door. She makes you jump.

"Wine," she says as she slides in. Somehow she holds up three bottles with just two hands.

The two of you are in your room, home alone. You lie on your bed, and your hair tickles the floor with your head leaned back. Roman paces beside you. Some mall-photoboothsnapshots of you and your best friend Kia in eighth grade are pinned to your wall. You two haven't talked in a year.

At the end of middle school, Kia's mom dropped you girls off at the movie theater on the edge of town. Kia invited Lonny, but of course, no one else knew. Lonny showed up ten minutes late and didn't sit in the same row as you. Asshole. Kia saw him as he entered though. She switched seats. Boos from the people around you. In a Kia fashion, she waved them off and started whispering in Lonny's ear. Even in the dark, you saw him grip her thigh.

"You know in prison," Roman starts. She brings prison up a lot, so you know a lot about it even though you've never been close to going. Even if you one-eighty'd and killed someone tomorrow, you'd still only end up in juvey. "I was raped," she finishes. She does this a lot, bring up big topics very casually.

You wonder if you're supposed to ask a question.

There's a box TV on your dresser in the corner but it's turned off. You've got a few pairs of jeans on the ground and a sweater hanging off the back of your desk chair.

She picks them up for you and cradles them in her arms. She adds, "It's fucked up how people are sent to prison for illegal shit, but the guards who work for the prison are allowed to do illegal shit. Like shove a woman's body in the dark, and lie against it like it's fabric. I told you. Everyone likes control and will play God if they have the chance." She throws your clothes in the closet. "Don't tell me God doesn't rape people."

Marker lines next to the doorframe show your growth over the years. Your mother stopped marking you sometime in early middle school. You're not sure if Roman thinks it's lame.

You say, "I'm sorry that happened to you."

She laughs in a way that sounds slurred. You're not sure how, but you know it is.

You know you sound stupid, but you don't know what else to say.

"Where's your mom?" She asks. She flops beside you on the bed. She's on her stomach. "Your dad?" She adds. She burps and doesn't apologize.

You don't know what she'll think if you tell her. If she'll look at you like a dirty little orphan.

Off your pink nightstand with stickers all over its side she pulls a beaded bracelet and starts chewing on it.

She urges, "Brothers? Sisters?" She shakes her hair out so it's spread down, touching the floor like yours. "God damn, tell me it's not you alone in this house, is it?"

What you hear her say is life ain't fair.

You start, "No brothers or sisters."

She rolls onto her side so her pinched nose faces your slender one, a mirror image of two different portraits.

You tell her your mother has worked a few jobs, sometimes at once.

"What kinda jobs?"

You hear one of the plastic beads break in half and she spits part of it out on the floor. She's wrapping the broken elastic around her wrist a few times until it snaps.

"She's saving people." She is the manager at a twenty-four-hour restaurant downtown.

Roman nods her head like she understands.

She looks at you and, real plain, she says, "You're kind of pretty, y'know that?" and you smile.

You think of the belly button ring you can't see since her stomach's flat on the bed and you think of the time you begged your mother for one. Your mother told you that you'd be scarred. No one would ever love you. You wouldn't get a job. Then she used the home computer to print out two newspaper articles, outlining piercing horror stories, that she left on your pillow for you to find the next day. They weren't even for the right type of piercing.

You wonder who pierced Roman.

She doesn't ask about your father again. She says, "Let's drink some wine" (turn to page 23).

You imagine the two of you swallowing happiness until you choke.

You decide on no to the church. That's not really your thing, but you tell her you can drop her off since it's halfway home.

You find an old bandage in the center cupholder when you get in your car. You're not sure where it has come from but you hope Roman doesn't see it. There's not really a way to take it out without calling attention to it now.

If she does notice, she doesn't say anything. She climbs into the passenger seat. She says fuck when she knocks her knee into the dash, and then puts her feet on top of it instead and rolls down the window. She twists her body so both her arms hang out of the car and she waits for her hair to whip. She reminds you of something helpless. Like a believer.

It's about a ten-minute drive to the church. You drive through the older, downtown historical district where there's only two lanes and many red-brick shops that are all connected. Green awnings cover the facades and a stray lab puppy with ribs shaped like cathedral arches weaves between street sign poles.

"You know in prison," Roman starts as soon as she sees the church up ahead. She brings prison up a lot, so you know a lot about it even though you'd never been close to going. Even if you one-eighty'd and killed someone tomorrow, you'd still only end up in juvey. "I was raped," she finishes.

You almost slam on your breaks, but stop yourself first. She's never told you this before.

The one stoplight up ahead is flashing yellow, so you slow down to make sure no one's coming sideways at you. The entire crossroad is empty.

You wonder if you're supposed to ask a question, but she picks up for you. She adds, "It's fucked up how people are sent to prison for illegal shit, but the guards who work for the prison are allowed to do illegal shit. Like shove a woman's body in the dark, and lie against it like it's fabric. I told you. Everyone likes control and will play God if they have the chance." She slams her hand still hanging out the window on the side of the car. It makes a tinny noise. "Don't tell me God doesn't rape people."

The church is centered in front of you now. A cathedral. Something pretty to look at.

You pull up to the drop-off point.

"I'm sorry that happened to you."

She laughs in a way that almost sounds slurred.

You know you sound stupid, but you don't know what else to say.

You park the car.

"I'm going to the gas station." She jumps out and starts walking across the street to a Shell station lit up in yellow. She looks over her shoulder and yells at you, "You comin'?"

You don't really want to, in addition to the fact you had planned on dropping her off and going home. But you've got no real excuse not to, so you turn off the car, hide the bandage in your pocket when she's not looking, and lock up. You promise her that you're on your way.

Roman's already inside when you get there. She's fussing with some Coke bottles in the fridge area, sneaking some chocolate bars off the shelf and down the waistline of her pants, leans over a mirror for sale to pick at something in her teeth.

You ask the guy at the counter if you can use the restroom. He practically throws you the key that's chained to a metal pole. If you couldn't catch, you'd have gotten smacked by the rod.

In the bathroom, you remember to empty your pockets. They're full of the things you tried hiding throughout the day. The bandage from the car. Your broken nail. A receipt for McDonald's.

Inside the trash can is some paper towel and a lot of other odds and ends. A bloody menstrual pad. A plastic orange juice bottle. A used condom. You're not sure if it was used here or somewhere else first.

The world is full of many secrets.

When you were a child, your mother would drop you off at your uncle's. She would work double shifts for three days in a row and the television might not be enough to watch you that long. She'd say goodbye, kiss you on the forehead, and let you walk yourself into the front door.

Your uncle had two kids, your cousins. One boy and one girl. You played Simon Says with them. One day your girl cousin got a hold of some scissors. She was four years old. The blades swished. She moved those handles so they'd slice straight through the air. The boy told her Simon Says cut something.

You watched her walk to the mirror. She raised the scissors so they were horizontal straight and parallel to her face. Any second and she'd have no more eyelashes. Snip snip.

The boy took the scissors, and she screamed.

Footsteps pounded.
Two reflections in the mirror rattled.
Scissors fell.

You didn't say anything when your uncle entered the room. The girl said that her brother hit her. You said nothing.

Your uncle was there for less than one minute before he grabbed the boy by the collar of his shirt and dragged him like a bag of sand. He threw him in the attached garage. Locked the door.

You heard your cousin scream and pound. Tiny fists make noises like rainstorms. The sound repeated until it didn't.

You heard your uncle yell to never touch sissy again or he'd fuck the boy up really bad next time.

The pounding stopped.

Your mother brought you back the next day.

The boy's been in and out of the hospital more times than you can count. Wrecked legs, snapped wrists, cracked ribs.

Adults are supposed to know it all. They're supposed to have all the answers, but no one ever gave them the answers. Who was the first adult? Who's the one to have known it all?

It's deceiving, thinking anyone won't make mistakes. We're all sinners, right. Some junk in the Bible says all sins are equal, too. We're all equally bad.

That's what Roman says, anyway.

She says that adults are just big kids. Big kids who never learned the word no. Because all sins are the same or something. Blah blah blah. That's what makes some people strong enough to survive and end up adults. And then they make more kids.

You wash your hands in the rusted, gas station bathroom sink and look in the scuzzy mirror covered in who-knows-what kind of stains when you hear pounding on the door. Roman screams to open up. You ignore her for a few seconds but she keeps pounding and sort of whispers that she'll scream like her life depends on it if you don't unlock that door in five, four, three, two –

Hands still wet, you open the goddamn door for her and she smiles. A small gap in her two front teeth beneath a dry, split lip.

You see the employee in the distance, behind her shoulder, staring at her ass. It makes you wonder if she stuck anything down that side of her pants.

She pulls you into her. Whispers in your ear, "Do you want to go to a party later?"

The words tickle your skin.

She adds, "Pretty please?" She's holding a bottle of Coke in one hand and a bottle of wine in the other.

You ask if she needs a ride and she says no. Not this time. She just thinks you'd have fun at a real party.

Really? That's it?

"Yeah." Then she smacks your butt.

You let the bathroom door swing shut and the gas attendant squawks for his metal rod back.

"All right girl, I'm goin' to church. I hope to see you later. Any time after nine. Or midnight if you want to look cool. I'll get you the address."

You almost tell her no (turn to page 48), you're just dropping her off here like you said you would and going to go home for the night, but then you think about how you've got nothing else actually going on later and it's not the church you'd be going to, so why not (turn to page 37).

Roman taunts, "Don't be such a baby." She sticks her tongue out at you as the gas station door shuts.

Now you're both lying so your heads are at the foot of the bed, and mostly Roman is drinking wine out of the bottle. Sometimes you take a sip. Sometimes she pours it in your mouth for you and you have no choice.

Roman says she's glad she got the wine.

You don't say anything.

"Ask me something." This is Roman's way of getting closer and it fucking terrifies you.

You stare at the immobile ceiling fan. You stare at the chain hanging from the immobile ceiling fan's lamp. You turn your head a little and stare straight into Roman's hungry eyes.

Fine.

"What did you think about when you were in prison?"

She doesn't hesitate. "Cocaine. Sex. If I had any money for "rent." If I was gonna pay "rent"- or if I'd rather just fight a bitch." You don't have to ask what rent is.

Then she asks what *you* think about while *you're* in prison, and it sucks that you know exactly what she means.

She adds, "If there's a god, he only keeps prisoners."

You don't say anything at first. Like usual. Does she even believe in God? And you're wondering what other things she thought of. Did she think of Valentine's Day? Her fifth-grade teacher? The boy next door? But Roman's not going to let you slide. She never ends with herself. She slips her finger lightly down your arm.

"I'm waiting."

"I don't have an answer."

She doesn't believe you, but she says, "Fine. Tell me a secret." You freeze.

"No thanks." You're awkward like kids are.

Roman liked to play hide and seek on you. She would disappear sometimes, but you'd know she hadn't left. You'd have to walk around your house, a place that you knew, and look at it like it was new all over again. Then you'd hear Roman. She doesn't breathe softly. When you would find her hiding behind the shower curtain, she'd gasp, "Shut up." She was the only one who ever told you to shut up. You'd ignore the noise she made. You'd tell her if she didn't want to be caught, she shouldn't have left the light on.

Lying there, so close to you, she reaches for your neck but misses and grabs your shoulders instead which she drags into her. You're practically nose to nose when she says, "Quit being a baby. Tell me a secret."

Then she reaches with one arm down the side of the bed, feels for something on the floor, and returns with the bottle of wine.

"This will help," she says matter-of-factly. The fingers on her free hand touch your lips. They're surprisingly soft as they trace your natural pout and pull it apart, and she awkwardly pours some wine into your mouth. It's splashing all over your face and the bed. You cough. She giggles. She says, "It will. Soon."

Your cough becomes a spit and you've stained your comforter red now.

"Okay, fine. I'll tell you one first."

You think getting raped in prison was enough, but you guess that's not much of a secret when she tells it to everyone anyway.

"My best friend for most my life was a dude."

"That's not a secret." Like you're one to talk though.

"Shut up, I'm not done." She tells you her best friend was a dude. Same age as her. They'd met in second grade? She doesn't know. Babies. They were babies, then she caught him fucking her sister right before graduation.

This feels like breaking a friend code, but you're not sure it's a secret.

Roman lifts the bottle of wine up to your lips and straight-eyes you like she means business. She tilts the bottle a bit and pours some in. You swallow hard.

She keeps talking. She says, "My sister is six years younger than me. She was, like, twelve at the time."

Oh. Wow.

"Yeah. I caught him slamming into her the week we finished school and I punched his face in. He didn't walk across the stage."

You've noticed that Roman gets giggly when she's drunk. From your experience, you think that's a good thing. You can't help but giggle with her.

"As far as I know, we're the only three who know about this." She rolled onto her back at some point, you didn't even notice, so you reposition yourself to stare back up at the ceiling too. You both stare at what is the solar system of your ceiling lamp. "Us three, and now you. Your turn."

You're feeling warmer. Softer. You can't tell if you like this feeling or not, but you do feel obligated to share something back.

Punching your best friend who rammed your little sister seems like a big enough deal. You'll give her that.

"The last time I got drunk," you start.

"Wait, you get drunk?"

"Used to."

She doesn't believe it.

You start over. Your eyes are closed so you can pretend you're somewhere far away and that you're not here with twenty-one-year-old Roman, or back there with this memory. You try telling yourself that you're somewhere new, which might not be so bad.

"The last time I got drunk, I did shots of vodka with friends." You don't tell Roman this was last year. Instead you complement her. "You seem like a fun drunk." Sweeten her up. You think it works because she laughs. "But I'm not a fun drunk. I'm not really mean, either. I just talk a lot." Your eyes remain closed. "Me and three others." You, your best friend Kia, and two girls you didn't really know. "And I ran my mouth a little too much. We'd all been drinking. Kia's an angry drunk though and she…" told the others about that secret. You were unsure of how to tell this to Roman. "…ran her mouth." You had been best friends since kindergarten and now you haven't talked to her since that night. You finish.

Roman pours the last of the wine in your mouth.

"That's why I don't really like drinking much anymore," you add, as a drop of it rolls down your chin.

"Fuck that." The words spill from Roman's mouth. "Was she pretty?"

"Who?"

"Kia."

You hesitate. "Yeah. She's the prettiest of anyone I know." You're slurring. Roman might have rolled her eyes.

"I've got an idea." She pushes herself up so she's now sitting on her knees. You're still lying on your back like a flopped fish out of water, looking at everything bigger than you, above you.

Roman shoves you around a little so your shoulder rolls into your center.

She says, "I want you to make a list of the prettiest girls you know."

You feel like vomiting.

Each one of the pretty girls flashes before your eyes like a countdown. You know, five, four, three, two, one – blast off.

You can tell that Roman can tell that you don't approve. It might be the teeth on your face. Showing a little. Lips too high.

She pouts, and her pout is so much better than yours, swollen and small. Delicate. Sexy.

"Will you do it?"

You think about where Roman falls on the list.

You wonder what she's thinking of, why she wants this list, and consider saying yes out of curiosity (turn to page 78), but you also know this sounds like a bad idea and want to just stand up to her and tell her no (turn to page 87).

She was always touching you like you were something special. Fingertips tapping the tops of your hands, smooth soft down the flesh on the side of your arm, a chin quickly nuzzled in your shoulder. These moments were always fleeting, never too long, but you noticed them. No one else had ever touched you like that except Kia, but Kia flirted with everyone.

Kia's a bitch.

Roman's shoulder-side is pressed against yours and she asks you if you've ever wanted to be close to someone. "Like, realllly close." She leans into your ear and whispers it. It feels inviting like secrets do. It's like she knows you're so far from being close to anyone. Like she knows you need it. She always has.

And your answer is yes. More than anything. Even if you won't tell her.

So you let Roman stay like that. In that position. She holds her pose so when you turn your head toward her, the tip of your nose is touching hers.

The response you give her is a diet version of the one you want to give, but you tell her yes. It would be nice to feel close to someone.

She smacks you on the back. You place a hand over your heart and cough.

She says, "Good."

She's got an idea.

Roman's full of ideas. You guess that must be what happens at that age. When you grow up.

When you were a kid, you thought older meant suffering. You watched your mother work day and night at blue collar jobs while you acted like a kid. Like a kid that others might finally like.

You thought older meant graduating from performance, because who was your mother performing for at that point? Performing was for kids, but after meeting Roman, you wonder if getting older is just more like playing God, with everyone's eyes on you. Even eyes from the people you're not paying attention to.

Roman's picked another scab off her knuckle, maybe the same one from earlier, and uses a finger to wipe away the blood. She smears it across her mouth like red lipstick. She puckers.

You don't say anything because it might be rude, and being rude doesn't get you far. You let Roman do whatever she's going to do.

"How old's your house?" She asks.

"I'm not sure. Fifty years old?"

"I think that's old enough."

"For what?"

Razor blades.

"What? What do you mean?"

You're still wondering what her plan for getting close is. She's still pressed against your shoulder.

A small fruit fly swishes past your faces. She uses her two hands to smash it immediately. Precise aim.

She asks if you've ever knocked down any walls in your house.

You say no.

She rubs the fruit fly corpse off on her jeans. There's a hole in the knee. You can't tell if it's a hole from wear or a hole that companies design before they sell them.

"Then you wouldn't know about the razor blades."

"What razor blades?" You repeat yourself.

"Ask me one more time."

What razor blades?

She looks straight at you.

She says, "Okay, okay. Fine. I'll tell you about the razor blades." She smiles. "There are people who have knocked down bathroom walls in older houses, just to find hundreds of rusty razor blades falling out of them. Imagine: a waterfall of razors."

"But why?" You hang on her words.

She tells you that the barber-shop-shit blades were too much work to use at home, so they made other, special razors that dudes could use in their own bathrooms instead. Razors didn't used to be in plastic like they are now.

You tell her you know. Does Roman think you're stupid?

"Okay, good. Because at first, people tried to throw these new razors in the trash. But you have to know that people burned the trash out back, and the razors would survive. Since they'd been thrown out in the garden and all, the gardeners had to worry about finding razor blades in there. Think about it: you're just picking carrots and you slice off a finger."

How dreadful.

Roman tucks hair behind her ear. It keeps falling in her face.

"So shit. Smooth-faced men had to get inventive. The new place to dispose of their razors (that kept smooth and kissable) was in their medicine cabinets, because these cabinets were fixed right to the walls. It was easy to just plop! Slip a razor in the cabinet and never think of it again."

Really? In the cabinet?

She says there was a convenient slit in the cabinet, which opened to the wall it hung on. So you put the little slicer in the slit, and it fell in the wall between the studs.

You imagine all the hiding spots people keep the tools that they want to destroy.

"Ya know what they called those new razors? Razors that were post-barbershop-travesties and pre-modern-day-plastic?"

What?

"Those razors, stacked up in walls, spilling out unexpectedly when the walls come down –

(pause for dramatic effect)

"They were called safety razors."

Instead of a wall full of razors, you think of a wall made of razors. This seems like a good way to keep people out. Most people don't like getting slashed open by a hundred blades.

Roman asks you, "Have you ever thought about drinking blood?"

And you immediately answer her no, because you haven't.

This is her idea of getting close.

She asks you why not and you tell her it didn't cross your mind because that's not what it's for.

She says, "Sure it is. It's meant to be inside us."

Celebrities do it.

Someone Roman knows who does it says it helps you to love another person for who they are.

You tell her you also don't like the taste of iron.

She says, "You know what else tastes like iron?"

You shake your head.

"A padlock, which locks something in. Like a secret." She adds, "I've never drank someone else's blood before. If we did this together, it could be our secret."

You're thinking about how, earlier, Roman told you that things aren't real.

But blood is real.

It has to be real. You can see it. Feel it. Taste it. Stain with it. It's real because you acknowledge it.

But now she's got you thinking.

Does blood exist?

You might have to acknowledge it to make it exist.

She shrugs her shoulder against yours and licks the red stain she had wiped there a while ago off her lips.

"See? Just a little bit. Not that bad."

You're not convinced.

"Would you do it," she sets her hand on your thigh, "for me?"

Maybe you could be.

"I wouldn't trust anyone else to do this with me."

Really?

The last time someone had said something like that to you was when Kia asked you to dump a hundred dollars' worth of perfume with her. My stepmom doesn't know the stuff smells disgusting, she said, and you girls needed to do her a favor. The two of you snuck her crystal bottles out to the storm drain on an evening Kia's dad took the lady out on a date. Kia told you about how she wore a mink jacket – you could still see little animal faces stitched in the front – to help you understand that this woman needed help. You were doing her a favor by tossing her trashy scent, and a small one at that. The spilled oil, splashed on concrete, smelt like leftover rain.

Roman's knuckle stopped bleeding in the middle of her talking, but she scratches it again to re-open the wound. She holds her hand out to you as if she wants you to kiss it like a gentleman would.

You say, "I don't have a scab."

"No problem. We can make your wound." She lowers her hand for now.

Bodies make seventeen million blood cells per second, and stress can produce up to seven times more of that amount. Thinking about blood stresses you out right now which means there's even more of it growing inside you.

Roman digs in her pocket before pulling something small and sharp out. It's not easy to tell what it is.

"Where do we do this?" You ask her.

She says there are no rules. It's up to you.

You think about where it will hurt the least.

You hold out your pointer finger and she takes it gently into her left hand, using her right to direct her weapon. As she brings it to your skin, it takes shape. It looks like a sharp animal nail.

"What is that?" You ask, pulling away.

Roman grabs your finger like she's a Chinese finger trap, keeping you in place, and calmly responds. "It's a claw."

"From what?"

"A cat."

She says cat claws are lucky, just like rabbit's feet. She asks if you've ever had a lucky rabbit's foot.

And you have. You carried the red thing around on a keychain with just your house key until you were twelve.

She says, "Cool."

Sharp things are all the same.

She releases your finger, holds it gently still in her left hand and with the nail that is already a little bloody in her right she scratches a quick cut on your finger.

"Practically painless, right?"

You nod your head with your eyes creased shut. Release a big breath from your nose. Those one-hundred-nineteen million blood cells race to the opening.

Roman's completely facing you now. She's practically sitting on top of you, her legs over yours, and her hands holding yours, she lifts your finger to her lips.

"You ready?" She asks. She sounds like she cares.

You nod your head.

Her soft woman lips press sweetly against your skin, even if it's just the knuckle of your finger. You think about how she might be your best friend. You think about telling her a secret. You don't. You think about promising her something. Normally, you would. But not now. Your other hand starts to twist some of the loose hair hanging on your shoulder while you feel her suck the blood from your body. She stops kissing your wound and adds some space between you two. She's again got some red smeared all over her heart-shaped lips but this time it's yours.

She wants you to be her lipstick.

That's all our bodies are – decoration.

She smiles at you and doesn't remove the blood.
She says, "Your turn."

She holds her bleeding hand out to you like before. You bend your face down so you're pressed against her, and take a quick breath like you've got to hold yourself underwater. You feel the veins and bones in her hand against your face.

With just the tip of your tongue you taste her blood.

And that's it.

It's done.

It tastes like metal. Something strong. Like a padlock.

Maybe it isn't that big of a deal.

She grabs your chin and raises you, like you've come up above the water. You choke on your own breath. You swallow. She swallows.

(Turn to page 65.)

You've got no idea where Roman's at.

The double door was cracked, so you invited yourself in.
You're not sure if that's custom, but you felt
    awkward,

                      uncomfortable,

         nervous

to call attention to yourself and knock. Besides, no one would
hear you. The music is loud.

                    What??

Sounds erupt around you, against you, they touch your
body. Montell Jordan's "This Is How We Do It."

The back of the door inside the foyer is almost barricaded
by people. Piles of people clot the inside of a home you will
never afford to own. Only a few try talking over the music
because the rest know that no one will hear them

                  between

    the music
    and people
    and living noises
    (living makes a lot of noise).

      The rest don't feel the need to be heard.

You want to find Roman.

It's late. There's a guy lying naked on the living room couch and the four people around him are shaving bits of hair off his body.

There's a girl bawling her little raccoon eyes out in the corner. Sticky sticky mascara. Dripping. She's got one girl patting her back. Her hair is in strings. Friend goes tap tap tap. It will be okay.

You tug your sweater down a little. You don't have a belly button ring like Roman. Your stomach's not cute enough, so you have nothing to show. You don't take off your shoes.

Someone walking by offers you a cup. Says he's so happy you're here and you can't tell if you are too or not. You take the cup – what else do you do at parties – and he runs into the wall that's in front of him.

You're not sure how old everyone here is.

There is a hallway straight ahead of you. The first door on the right opens. Your red cup's splashing as you get knocked into. You haven't drunk any of it yet. Someone walks out of the open door. He's got round eyes, an angled jaw, and a sports jacket paired with Converse. He's grinning, looks at you, winks. He might've winked at three other girls too but you bite your lip and can't get past it.

You're wearing a ring on each finger. Some thin and fake rose gold, some chunky, some sterling silver. Mixed and matched. This is in style this season, or maybe last season. You don't know these things. You tried to plan out being cool before coming.

You start to weave through the crowd to figure out where Roman's at, but the boy walks up to you. He says to you, "I'm Humphrey and you're Lauren." You don't know that these names belong to some iconic, movie star couple. He adds, "What's our story?"

Another boy walks by – might be a man – gives you a thumbs up.

You stare at him uncertainly. Your mind empties but the room is busy. You suddenly don't know how to be yourself.

      Music pounds.

      Wasted woman screeches.

           Another girl glares at you.

Sobs from corner.

    Is that a dog barking?

More vodka.

More beer.

         Upstairs, want to

         go

Yap yap yap.

"You've got ten seconds, go."

The cute boy's in front of you, almost chest to chest. No personal space.

You say, "We met on a train." You say this because you've never been on a train.

He says, "I like that. Adventurous."

You say, "We got off at the wrong stop." You add, "Together."

He says, "We hold on."

You say, "To the train." Like you made a mistake getting off. Need to get back on. Certainly not holding each other. Guys like hard to get.

The boy taps your cup. Almost falls over. Asks what you're drinking.

You don't know.

MC Hammer's "U Can't Touch This."

He lifts your cup, takes a sip, you haven't even yet. You notice small bits of powder above his lip. Under his nose. Right where it belongs. The door the boy walked out of opens once more.

It's Roman. Of course.

    Music crashes
Splatters   pops
A popping noise from beer pong
You want to sip the drink
        What is it?
Roman giggles
Holds a girl's hand
    She dragged out
        The boy falls into you
Just a little
    Two men carry their friend
    Out the door.

You tell the boy to have a great night. You haven't even left the doorway yet.

Roman's practically lying against the hallway wall, if you can do that standing up. Mouth wide open, still holding hands with the other girl. Woman. She looks like a woman. Which makes sense because Roman's some kind of woman too. You inch your way through the clot. The crowd. You spot Roman really close to her, skin near skin, breath on skin, she's putting an earring in the girl's/woman's ear.

You take a sip of your cup. Don't know what it is. It tastes strong. You cough. You spit. You drink. Drink more. You hear a whine. Roman's laugh. She puts the backing on. Says, "There there."

You say, "Roman."

She turns to you and smiles. "You showed up!"

Your face flushes. You nod. Up down up down.

She introduces you to the other woman. You ignore her. You want to ask her, don't want to, kind of want to, don't ask her what you're supposed to do here. You don't know anyone.

You hear Roman giggle again. The freckles on her nose dusted white. She's being dragged down the hallway, her free arm stretched out to you like a telephone wire disconnected. She's too far to touch. Giggling.

Backstreet Boys' "I Want It That Way" is playing loudly somewhere.

You get left alone. The hallway light's bulb is out so it's covered in shadows except for dim sights made visible by the foyer light across from you, the living room lamp to the right and the kitchen light on the left. There's at least eight people you can see around you and there's more in other rooms, other halls. You're next to the door the others had opened. It's shut now. Will open again soon. Behind it will be white lines, leftover lines, powder, on the sink and back of the toilet. You hear someone scuffle behind the door.

Everything feels like it's happening in slow motion.

A woman, much older than everyone else, walks past you, then back to you, up to you. She has slicked blond hair the length of a mother's. She has an infinity tattoo on her bicep. Her bicep is quite round. She asks you how old you are.

Another door down the hallway opens. Two people walk out. Pants unzipped. That's supposed to be in season now too.

Momma asks you again, but she's clearly been drinking. She doesn't know the difference between sixteen and thirty-four right now. You tell her twenty-five. Her nails are painted red.

When you were six and your grandmother died, your mother stopped taking on extra shifts for a while. She never told you she stopped, but sometimes people's choices are obvious. Even without sharing the truth.

She'd come home from work. She'd have liquor breath. Her nails were always red.

This is when the television was your babysitter.

The times she actually worked double shifts were when your uncle was your babysitter.

Both times were damaging.

You wished your mother had had a man in her life. Maybe then things would've been different.

You're cornered off alone in the hallway. Almost finished with your drink. You notice one of your rings is missing. It was too big. You think you see a man drag his feet down the hall, but then you can't see anyone. Maybe there was no man.

You end up in the living room. There's beer pong happening behind the couch. Two people on the couch. Lying there, tongues in mouths, connecting, ignoring.

Your cup is empty. You set it on a coffee table. The group playing beer pong has a few cups left.

You don't know where Roman is. Something Jennifer Lopez is playing.

You walk over to beer pong and pick up a cup sitting on their playing field. Whatever it is. You don't know what they call it. Your eyeliner has started smearing but you don't even know. You start to walk away.

Someone playing at the table calls to you. Was that a bark?

You turn. He's a man, at least ten years older than you. Probably more.

He yells too loudly again. "Hey, come back here."

Your skirt is inching up and you don't want to pull it back down.

"You gonna give that back?" He asks you.

"I wasn't planning on it." You take a sip and try not to gag.

He says, "All right, well," and lifts his hand holding onto a ping pong ball and drops it in the drink. He swipes the cup from you and takes a full swallow and adds, "Save some for me."

You breathe in through your nose. You look at the white t-shirt he's wearing tucked into his Levi's and he looks too cool for this place. He's got some sort of boots on that make it look like he's good with his hands. He presses his arm with a wristwatch into the small of your back before he turns away and yips at his opponent. Claims he's going to beat his ass and win. Something about that sounds reassuring to you.

You used to sit in your bedroom while your mother sat in the bathroom. Smoking a joint. Your mother, that is. She'd sit on the toilet with her legs stretched out so her feet rested on the tub, and she'd try to smoke so that it blew out the small shower window. Sometimes too much smoke triggered the smoke detector.

She wouldn't even bother waving a towel at the alarm to stop it. Just let it shriek until it was finished. There was no emergency.

Eventually she took the smoke detector down.

You're sitting on a couch in the basement. You don't know how you got down here. You're alone. You've stopped paying attention to songs. You haven't talked to Roman all night, and she's the one who invited you here. You haven't seen that Humphrey character. Don't want to talk to Momma. You're nursing your third or fourth cup of something and wishing someone was looking for you.

Beer pong man is suddenly next to you. He smiles at you and you want to vomit. Bad light down here. Couch is sagging. Mustard yellow. Is this your fifth cup? He asks why you took his beer game. Game beer. Pong cup. You don't know what he says. You took it.

"I needed more alcohol," is what you say to him.

"I understand." He doesn't try and touch you.

"I need to feel something."

One time your mother told you that you needed to lose weight. How disappointing, overwhelming, like you were/are/ too much space. She patted your knee and told you that you two never talk anymore. She just doesn't know how to talk to you.

"What does something feel like?" He asks.

The man's name is Evan. He has to know you're a kid, but he calls you a beautiful woman. He says you're very interesting.

"Real."

You don't know what time it is, but you two have been talking for a few hours. It feels like that. In out in out around people have moved. A couple sat next to you, made out against Evan's back. A burly guy stumbled down the stairs before someone helped him up.

Roman who?

"Why do you feel so… fake?"

You can't decide if it's fake or nonexistent.

"What I feel is like I have been awake for weeks. I feel like there is no off button. I feel like everyone will watch me spin, even if I don't want them to." You think about it. "Or maybe they won't. That might be scarier. That I couldn't stop spinning, and no one knew. No one watched."

He lets you sit. Evan doesn't ask you to do it, or pull you into him, but you shrug against his shoulder where this man feels warm. He wraps his other arm around you.

He asks you why you feel that way and you tell him it's a long story. He says he's willing to listen. Instead, you rub your hand along his arm just to feel his skin. Your fingers are like rain, they run downward, and then you almost work your fingers between his before you realize for the first time he's got a ring, like you have rings. You almost say that you're twins before you realize what gold bands mean on men. On their ring fingers.

You say, "You're married?"

You try to push yourself away but you can't.

"I'm in an open relationship," he tells you. He doesn't ask if you know what that is.

"How?"

He chuckles. Not at you maybe, but at something. He says that there are so many moments, chances, in the world that we miss when we belong to someone. Like this. This moment with someone like you. He'd never want to miss it.

In just a few hours at a house party, he managed to be the lie in the word believe.

"It's different, I know. But it's okay, I promise."

He promises.

You wonder what he thinks of your makeup.

You're reminded of how your mother used to wear blue eyeshadow. Now she wears eyeliner and lipstick.

People will believe in others before they believe in themselves. People will believe in God before they believe in others.

From behind the couch you're sitting on with Evan, Roman pops up and shouts boo.

She doesn't scare you, although like a ghost she seems to haunt you.

She drops a giggle. Her hair is a knot. She's got a small drop of blood under her nose. "Oh, your necklace."

You put it on before you left. She sits on top of your lap, nearly on top of Evan's lap, and uses her fingers to untangle your chain. She smooths it out along your neckline and pats it down.

You don't ask where she's been all night.

"I hope you have fun." She says this like you aren't sitting next to someone else.

You think she may mean had fun.

"Can I ask you something?"

Of course she can ask you something. She says this like there could be any other answer.

She whispers in your ear in a way that Evan can still hear, "It's important."

She's sloppy as she asks, "It's getting late. Can I come back to your place?"

It's frustrating that she bailed on you the whole night. You want to say no and talk more with Evan (turn to page 142). You like the way he listens. But you also know that Roman might end up in trouble if she stays here by herself. You should probably just take her home (turn to page 65).

Before you answer, she says, "Let me try on your rings."

You take your clothes off in front of the mirror sometimes. You are not sure why. It's not to love the way you look, but it's not to hate yourself either.

Everyone could be happy.

Now is not one of those times.

You are fully dressed, in front of the mirror, applying makeup. First, you cake your face in cover up. Something that matches your skin, but better. You read somewhere that you're supposed to put some sort of lotion or cream on underneath, but you can't afford that and you're not doing this for Vogue.

Your Pixies album plays behind you.

You wipe on eyeshadow. Bold move, after the face stuff, because now you've got eyeshadow dust all over your cheeks. You have to wipe it all off and start over.

You spend the next two hours putting makeup on. Again and again.

Your cheeks blush almost perfectly.

You used to ask your mother to watch episodes of Forensic Files. She'd say yes, but only if you'd keep your mouth shut. You promised you would. You squished together on the La-Z-Boy recliner, the only piece of furniture in the living room, in a way that mothers and daughters should. Might. Sometimes do. Your mother kept a sweaty Bud Light in her hand the entire time. Your eyes stayed focused on the images taking shape on screen, waiting for the climax.

When it finished, you went to your bedroom and re-enacted the murders with your dolls.

"And then Barbie stabbed Skipper nine times in the kitchen." You narrated the whole scene. You described the death. What ended up in the files. Barbie's plastic hand violently knocked against the other doll. Your aim missed, and the pointed arm ran right into your hand holding Skipper instead, and you started to bleed.

Your mother was asleep on the couch.

Maybe it was better that way.

Keep on pretending.

You turn your face so you get a look at yourself from a different angle. Pout your lips. Is this sexy? Is this what boys like?

You're pressed up against the mirror. Flattening your cleavage. Using your hands to push your tits together, to emphasize it again. You push your jaw out. The mirror is floor-length. You sit down on your knees. Or up on your knees. Down up. Up down. You're still pressed against your reflection, ready to fuck yourself like a lover would.

You kiss the glass, pretending to breathe softly, tenderly, some kind of way that shows a guy you love him. Then you back away and realize your lipstick has left a mark.

Roman has tried explaining to you what sexy is. She can do this because she is sexy, in the one pair of jeans she owns, tops that fit a little too tight, belly button ring she's worn since sixth grade, and no makeup usually. Still, she is sexy, so what she tells you must be true. Sexy doesn't come from your family, she said. Her dad is deadass a fat slob who wears the same wife beaters she does when he's not preaching, her mom lines her eyes with outdated, electric blue pencil, and her sister has sex but isn't sexy. She's more like a male honeybee, Roman has said. The honeybee's only job is to mate with the queen – just once though. When he fucks, his testicles are ripped apart. The queen stores his semen for later.

The whole honeybee situation sounds way more like what men do to women though, so maybe Roman's sister is more like an antechinus, a little mouse-looking creature, who has sex for up to fourteen hours at a time. But the sister has short hair like a boy and coughs without covering her mouth. Roman says, sexy doesn't come from genes.

"Where Is My Mind?" starts playing, and you think about how Kia was the one who gave you this album.

This song played a year ago while you, Kia, and two girls you barely knew took vodka shots in front of your dresser mirror. Joanie brought it. You didn't ask how she got it. You just drank. Everyone had told their parents that you girls were attending an away football game that night, and each girl got permission to stay over at your house after. You never went to the game, and no one told their parents that your mother would not be home.

You're not a happy drunk or an angry drunk, but you found out that you run your mouth a little too much.

So you went on, went on, went on

       and on

on   on   on

on and on

and on   and   on

on about

the way you thought your period was too long compared to other girls', and how you thought you made the neighbor's dog sick and almost killed it, and that the girl at school who everyone thought had really cute eyes just looked like a bug, and how do you ask someone to have sex, and then finally, you brought up how Kia's dad was on the sex offender list.

Sometimes accidents are dramatic.

Kia lost it (she is an angry drunk). She stood up on the bed, wobbling in a way that almost made her fall, and said she had an important announcement she wanted to make. She looked you in your face and thanked you for reminding her of it. She turned to the other girls then and told them, "You should never go to a doctor." See, her dad was a doctor, and the types of people who do what her dad did are the same people who end up as doctors.

You knew she wasn't criticizing her dad though. She kept going. You can still imagine her heavy breath and the way she spit against each word.

She told the room about the time you two were nine. She said your mother would drop you off for weekends at a time with nothing but the clothes on your back and, maybe, a toothbrush. The girls imagined you broken. Poor. Homeless. Her mom would dress you in a Little Mermaid nightgown and cook you roast beef. She'd make you popcorn for the Friday night movie – it was tradition. And then, when her mom would wish the both of you a good sleep as you lay under the blankets on Kia's bed, Kia told the girls, you would ask her to play doctor. You always directed her to be the patient. Kia asked if they all knew what that meant. She just wanted to make sure. She took more vodka shots. She slammed the bottle. She told them that you know what her pussy feels like.

"Which means you know exactly how to ask for sex," she screamed at you.

Now these other girls, woozy from vodka, knew your secret. You tried to puzzle, to piece together, what would win them back. Make them forgive you.

The answer was nothing.

Kia started sobbing and the girls pet her back, hugged her, whispered something unintelligible in a way that kept you out. You picked up the Nintendo controller you had borrowed for that night and asked them to play with you, but they were busy whispering secrets they'd never share. Kia nodded her head.

Tiny curls bouncing. A mole above her lip. No collarbones. Kia was a little girl. Not sexy. Pretty though. Prettier than you.

She hasn't talked to you since. You still have her Nintendo and Skip-Bo.

Girls are taxes.

Women are city limits.

You notice a stack of cheap rings on your dresser. You only own cheap things. You have a lot of rings. Your mother has necklaces.

You wonder what you look like with them on. You think this as, one by one, you slide them onto your slender fingers. Most of them are plain, fake, rose gold. Some of them are chunky. A few are stainless steel. You consider switching them around. You use them interchangeably, as girls must learn to do.

Girls are spiteful.

While Kia never spoke to you again, Luca did. Luca wasn't cute, with his sweat-wet hair and oily-pimple face, but he had nice lips and silver-dollar eyes. You told Kia one time about the dream in which you kissed him.

In the dream, it was late. You and Luca were at the mall together. This was strange because you'd never been to the mall with Luca. Never had any kind of hangout with him for that matter. You weren't even sure he knew you existed in real life, but in this dream, an announcer came on the overhead speakers reminding guests, "The mall closes in fifteen minutes."

Suddenly, things were urgent. Fifteen minutes was all you had left with the boy before you'd have to call home to your rides and make your way back.

Instead of finding the front doors to leave, he took you somewhere deeper in the mall. Dark. Small. Maybe a bathroom. Maybe a closet.

The problem is that this dream with Luca is one of those dreams where you remember it happened, but you don't remember how. So kissing Luca was a possibility, probably in some corner of that close-to-empty building, but you'd never get to relive the rush of lips against lips with him because it's all now just a blur.

You figure he might have rushed you hard against the wall. Sometimes you imagine his hands pushing yours up above your head. Hearts hearts hearts. It never crosses your mind to think about how he might have swallowed your mouth like underclassmen do, leaving you desperate for air, and you might not have even liked it.

Then he walked up to you at lunch in real life and asked if he could sit by you. He said, "Sorry, there's just nowhere else to sit," but you knew that was a lie. There were at least six other spots open, and four of them were at tables with boys.

You thought that maybe your dream was coming true.

The bell rang. Mrs. Shepard waved kids out of the lunch room. Yelled that it's time to learn. A mind wasted means she has to live with a bunch of morons in her old age, she shouted at the kids who left milk cartons on the tables.

Luca said he had to go. "Besides Mrs. Shepard yelling, I've got a test. But do you want to meet up by the baseball bleachers after school?" It wasn't baseball season.

You nodded your head and your frizzy hair bounced with it. Even in your baggy sweatshirt and tussled ponytail, Luca Sartowski wanted to make out with you. It was no dark corner of a closing mall, but your dream was coming true.

You waited by the bleachers for an hour. You sat. Watched the ladybug land on the metal next to you, resting in the bleacher's groove. You counted the spots on its wings. Eleven.

What if he was just running late? What if something horrible happened?

He wasn't. It didn't.

The next day at lunch, Luca sat at a table full of boys. He had no problem finding a seat that day. He ignored you, but the table Kia had started sitting at, a group of girls who were chronically late to school, dissolved into laughter when you walked past them to grab plastic silverware.

"Did you get a kissss?" Anne Marie, one of the girls from your bedroom, cooed at you.

The most you could do was ignore her. Adults tell children that's what you do when another kid's being mean. Ignore them.

This does not stop anyone from being mean.

Adults must be liars. After all, they're just big kids, and no one ever gave them the answers.

But teenage girls are ruthless. That's why Roman never wants to have any.

Roman told you that in prison she started puking. At first, she couldn't figure out why. She wasn't sick, and she didn't eat much, so there wasn't even a ton that came out. After a few weeks of keeling over from nausea and hiding out from other inmates so she wouldn't get pummeled for being weak, she found out she was pregnant.

She thought she was pregnant with a girl. She will swear up and down to you that it was a girl. The energy inside her was volatile which meant that's the only thing it could be.

She told you that was the worst thing that could ever happen to her. Times two. Being pregnant and the child being a girl. She wanted it gone.

Roman's told you that you can get abortions in prison, but it costs money, and you don't have money when you're in prison. At least not enough to take care of your body like that when you're a woman. It's like people think they're punishing the scum of the Earth by forcing them to carry parasites.

You're not sure if she actually told you that last part or if you're just thinking of it now.

She's said she could have threatened the guard, but she wanted to live. Just without a little girl, so she took care of it herself. She tells you if abuse yourself, that's all it takes. She punched her abdomen hard enough and now she's baby-free.

Still naked in front of your mirror with a full face on, you reach over to open the bottom left drawer of your dresser. Inside, there is nothing but the things you hide. A plastic bag of hair you chopped off a few years ago without your mother knowing, the key to a journal you keep inside the air vent underneath your bed, a drawing of a naked man that looks like he could be the lead singer of any of the bands you like that you bought from a kid in homeroom, and your electric toothbrush covered in dried cum. You reach across these things until your fingers find the yellow disposable camera.

It's nearly a year old and still has five pictures left to take. You aren't sure what's on the first half now, but the last few include your feet with hot pink toenails strapped in a pair of navy-blue stilettos you put on at the thrift store. You did not buy them. There's also a closeup of just your lips, splintered but shut, painted in a coral color you stole from the drugstore.

You put on a bra. It's black and kind of shiny. It's not silk, but you think it's the sexiest bra you own since the others are mostly jersey bras and have doodle graphics of dinosaurs on them. Kia's seen you in those before.

You put on a skirt that's hard to keep down. Your mother gave it to you as a late gift for a holiday she forgot about.

You hike your right foot up on the dresser so your girlish hips and thighs face their own reflection. You place the camera's backside against the mirror so it's easier for you to guess the angle it will capture. You shake your head, tousle your hair, and lean forward. The hills of your chest are minimal, so you curl your shoulders to emphasize them. Your upper arms now look fat. You pull your shoulders back and just use your hand to push your tits up instead. Pixies still play somewhere behind you. You snap the first picture, intending it to be full body. You didn't put the flash on so it will probably not turn out. You tilt the camera down – full body with no head. You lift the camera toward you – a peak at what your skirt barely envelopes. The next is the same shot but lower, and you're glad you've got the flash on now because, otherwise, your body creates too much of a shadow at that angle and it would never turn out. The fourth picture faces the mirror – you've climbed on top of the dresser so both your knees sit hard against the surface, you lean back on your feet as much as you can without falling off so your legs create a V, and you arch your back. You take the picture and the flash goes off. In the mirror, this will certainly eclipse you. You don't take the last photo.

You first took photos up your skirt behind the movie theater with Daria and some boys two summers ago. You know Daria from the before-school latchkey program you attended as a kid where she cut the shoe laces off of some boy's sneakers. Sometime after Kia left, Daria asked you to the movies while you two were hiding out in the locker room during gym class. You figured why not. She told you to wear a skirt.

You walked a mile to the local theater that's built with cinder blocks and little, yellow marquee lights. Three boys you didn't know stood around Daria as the popsicles they held dripped down their wrists, but she waved when she saw you anyway.

She introduced you to the group and one of the boys said, "Nice skirt." Daria had her own skirt on too, plaid.

"I promised the guys they could have some fun." She handed you a disposable camera and said, "Take some pictures."

The first boy stretched out on the parking lot concrete in front of Daria's feet. His buck tooth grin pulled his cheeks wide apart the moment you asked, "Now?" Daria nodded her head. Mhmm.

Then the boy threw his head back, staring at the space between her thighs. He said, "Oh yeah," and she winked at you but kept her eye closed longer than normal.

"Are you gonna take the picture or what?"

"Oh – of this?"

"Well, duh," the boy said. The others laughed.

Daria added, "What did you think I meant when I said now?"

You pressed the little black button and the flash went off.

"All right, next!" Daria shouted.

A greasy man walked out of the theater's back door and scattered your whole group like marbles. The three boys ran around the corner, you turned to face the other direction, and Daria just stood there. He tossed a large trash bag out in the dumpster kitty-corner to the building and never even looked at you.

When all three boys got pictures of their faces up Daria's skirt (which took less than two minutes) she asked, "How about you let them at it now?" She said the boys might appreciate some more fun.

You thought about the way the mound of flesh underneath her clothes, one just like yours, was like the meat of a lemon. Soft, pulpy, and bitter. You had watched the hunger in those boys' eyes as they waited in line for her, their tongues stained red from popsicles. They must have imagined peeling her apart and tasting her with their open mouths. They probably prayed she would fill them up and alleviate their appetites. Something about this felt ardent and urgent and you wanted nothing more than to control the feeding of this kind of human desire.

You said yes.

The front door opens and your mother drops her keys on the floor. You hear her walk to the kitchen, open the fridge, walk back down the hall, and sit on her bed to eat what's probably a cold, leftover rendition of some discount boxed macaroni and cheese.

You climb down from your dresser as a wild animal might, and you nearly trip and break your ankle, stumbling forward into your spring mattress instead. You know that falling like that would be an unflattering pose to be found in and an even worse story to tell.

You can hear your mother cackling to something. You consider shutting your door and getting wine drunk in your bra with a bottle that Roman slipped you as you left the gas station (turn to page 61), or you change your mind and go to the party she invited you to after all (turn to page 37).

You face the mirror square on in your bra and skirt and makeup. You hate the way you look.

What will get you noticed?

You don't finish putting clothes on. Why bother. You still hear your mother in her bedroom, the kitchen, the bathroom, somewhere else, even though you shut the door. The rooms in the house are close, and insulation isn't good.

You're sprawled out on your bed. Right now you're on your stomach, leaning on your elbows, holding the bottle of wine in front of you, but you're not sure the best way to do this. Should you sit up? Lie on your back under the blankets? You just want to see what happens. Then you realize that wine bottles need corkscrews.

You look around your room. Box TV on a wooden dresser. Nightstand covered in stickers. A ten-dollar full-length mirror against the wall. A ratty rug on the hardwood floor. Photos of you and girls who you haven't spoken to in at least a year and Seventeen Magazine pages of celebrities you'll never talk to taped to your walls. Then you notice a wire hanger poking out from under your closet door.

In fifteen minutes, you've managed to deconstruct your hanger and hook the cork with it. Your mother probably heard the popping noise, but she also might not care.

Your Pixies album repeats itself. This is probably the fourth repeat. You've taken a few sips already and while you don't like the taste, this wine is easier to drink than some of the other, harder alcohols you've tried in the past.

You're drinking straight from the bottle so you don't know how many glasses you've had. Maybe one or two, but it also seems like people don't fill wine glasses completely, so that type of measurement might change the number you think you've had. Maybe more?

You don't feel drunk. Unless you are and just unaware of it, which is terrifying.

You keep drinking, unsure of when you plan to stop. You shouldn't drink the whole bottle, but you also don't feel anything yet. Maybe you need to drink more.

Then you decide you're not drunk, but you feel light. Soft. Like you're barely on top of the covers of your bed now. You haven't felt good like this in a while, and you enjoy the feeling. You know you shouldn't take any more drinks, but you can see why people might like getting drunk, so you do. It's nice as long as you don't spill all your secrets to your friends, strangers, people in your bedroom. Whatever they are. You let a small laugh go because you're starting to lose your thoughts.

It might be time to try meeting people.

You want to see who you like when you're drunk. You also think about how it might be nice if others were drunk when they first met you. It might make liking you easier.

It's like eight or nine o'clock at night.

You remember, there was a day when you sat in a booth in the back of Leo's Coney Island, where you and Roman had gone before. In this memory you are alone. You were drinking vanilla milkshakes with no whipped cream and snapping rubber bands against your wrist. You were looking out the window next to you, watching customers like they were a videotape on rewind where they entered the building, and then went back to the car. Back and forth.

Your mother had been missing for three days. On another day she'd come home, but you didn't know that yet. Roman had been spending the week at her man's place.

You tried flagging the waitress down. This meant waving your hand softly, then more violently, so that it almost started looking like a signal flag. She didn't see you.

If you're going to go date people, meet people, exist with people – whatever the word is you're trying to come up with – you'll need to go outside.

You try standing, walking. You're in front of your mirror and you don't think you're drunk but you look a little more sideways now. You decide that you look even less attractive than you normally do, which isn't saying much.

You're still in a short skirt and a bra and don't see the point of putting on any other clothes. There's no point when you are just a transition.

You feel light and good but you also feel like crying. You don't want to mess up your makeup though. You tried so hard to make it perfect and if you cry it will destroy your hard work. Then what's the point?

You pull out your phone. You dial a number. Sorry, you misdial a number. You call an old woman sitting on her living room couch with a bowl of traditional Lay's potato chips and a cat on her lap and she asks who you are, why you are calling so late. She says you're lucky she's not in bed yet you'd have woken her up.

You apologize more than you need to, tell her you didn't mean to. You hang up without telling her that's what you're doing.

You try dialing again and this time get Roman. It's loud behind her. There are people. There are people paying attention to others, you think.

Hello, she asks.

You aren't sure if you've said anything yet.

You say hi back, so she knows you're there.

You don't know how late it is. You don't have clocks in the house or you don't look at the time. But you figure it's time for her to leave wherever she is soon.

You ask her if she wants to come over to your place. You say, "I'll pick you up." You think she says yes. It's hard to hear. You tell her you'll grab her in a little bit (turn to page 65).

You almost leave without clothes before you realize it. When you pass your mirror you notice bare skin in the reflection. You tell yourself that no one wants to see you stripped down and you put a shirt on backwards.

The two of you are sitting in the unfilled dark and Roman asks, "Have you ever noticed how the moon's shape appears to change each night?"

You can't decide if you have.

She says that, to the people who pay attention, it does. It's not always a full moon, is it?

Oh, no. You feel dumb.

"The reason it's constantly different is because the sun only lights up parts of it while it's orbiting Earth, depending on where things are positioned. So when all of those elements change, different parts get lit up." She pauses. "It's not the moon changing. Just our view of the moon."

You don't know Roman's other friends too well. It's mostly just you two. But sometimes she tells you about Tina who is one of the other four or five women who you know stay at the same drug dealer's house that Roman does. Tina is called a slut on the regular – rightfully so. And you guys make fun of Jerome, who is one of the drug dealer's guy friends that she sometimes hangs around, and how he is the one who got Tina called a slut. No one ever called him that. (Roman says sex makes people stupid.)

So you know you're not the only one she spends time with, but sometimes it feels like it.

Sometimes you tell her about Kia. What life was like with her. About how you'd call her to talk, even after you had just left her house, and that you were able to just walk into hers, even if she wasn't home. Then Roman would say, "Other animals don't do this to themselves." You stopped telling her about Kia.

"Why don't you talk about your dad?"

Roman's full of questions.

"There's not much to say about him I guess."

"I bet that's not true."

You can't see her well in the dark, but you're sure she's facing you, expectantly. As if, suddenly, you have something to say about him that maybe you didn't before. There's really nothing to say about him.

"Well, he's not here, is he?"

"So where is he?"

You close your eyes so the dark is darker, and start running your fingers through stringy parts of your hair.

"I don't want to talk about it."

"I don't care."

Roman is selfish.

She scoots so the space between you two is smaller. You're not sure if you like it. You think you do, but does it come with a price?

"What happened?" She asks again.

You're not even sure and that's partly why you don't discuss it.

You admit to her that you don't know. Truthfully. Your parents never married. You think you're the result of your mother dating the same guy for a few weeks, but that guy, your father, didn't really want a kid.

Telling Roman this feels like a promise.

You tell her, "He stuck around anyway, although I think he wanted a boy."

You remember how, years ago, you sat on your front step with one shoe on and one shoe off. The mailbox on a wooden pole was bent funny and the flowerbox was full of weeds. One weed had a flower budding. You were five. Your mother came out to you, sat down next to you, and told you that your father wasn't coming back. He was gone. You didn't know where or why.

Then your grandmother died shortly after. "Things got really rough around here."

Roman's got something to say. "Fuck men."

It was your mother's fault though.

Roman's definitely staring at you now and you wish she'd stop. "How?"

Your breathing is shallow. Your chest is skintight. Telling this story feels like someone staring at your growth over the years marked off in pen on the wall.

Your mother always said she had no idea where he went, or what he was doing. She didn't know why he left, and she did her best to protect you. But then you found out he was in jail.

"Oh shit."

You tell Roman that your mother sent him there.

"That's some crime show material." Roman's voice is too loud.

He stopped paying child support and the courts did nothing about it, so your mother called the cops because she knew he had forged his father's will.

She knew exactly how to destroy him.

Your throat feels tight like a rubber band, about to snap.

"He had the money. He could have paid her, and he wasn't," you add. "So the cops arrested him on forgery. And now that he's out, he wants nothing to do with us, so it's like he disappeared for real."

Roman might say it's almost like he doesn't exist.

You watch her lips purse, her cheeks pulled taut. She's quiet. Roman's usually coarse, matter-of-fact, and full of information. She's a woman and she knows it. This is unusual for her.

To cut the silence, you add, "I guess, to be fair, he'd been doing illegal things."

Making excuses is easier sometimes.

"I found all this out last year. Right after Kia bailed."

Roman's told you before that people who want kids are selfish. The people who think they *have* to have families. The people who need to have "their own" families so bad that they spend thousands of dollars and tons of hours at fertility clinics (four in ten adults say they've used fertility treatments) just to have their own parasites. And it's not for any bigger good or anything. It's selfish, because no one asked the kids if they wanted to be here. To deal with all this shit they're going to have to deal with. No. The parents think it's necessary to have them, but then most of them end up like Roman. Or you. Then what?

You feel like clawing your skin and pulling off the pieces. Then you might swallow every last bite. You want to devour yourself, leaving nothing behind.

You never wanted to tell anyone that story. You need wine.

Roman tells you that dads and moms are walking mistakes. Sometimes you forgive them and sometimes you don't.

We put all this faith in them when we're kids, trusting that what they tell us is real because we're stupid. Like what they say is rule, because they tell us it is. (Then she adds, that's why people believe in God, which is just further proof that we're all dumb as shit.)

And then we grow up and realize that they aren't smarter than us. We're the same as them. And that just shows us that we're the ones coming up with all the answers. We can answer things ourselves.

Roman told you that she dated a guy once. You think she's probably dated more than one, but she told you about the guy she dated last before being sent to prison. He was the kinda guy who'd call a girl "Darling." She said he was lanky, thin as a rod, but he was tall and that made up for it. Said she had no issue dating thin men if they were tall. If they were short and thin, she felt like she was going to crush them.

After she got convicted, she never reached out to him again. She figured there was no point. If she wasn't one before, she could definitely never be a darling after that.

And then, no warning, she spits at your face, wet and sticky, dripping down your cheek, and laughs. It's a deep, real laugh. She's not quiet about it.

You're smacking, wiping, smearing her saliva off your cheek. "What's that for?"

Instead of answering you, she spits again.

You think, if it was anyone else, you'd call them absolutely disgusting, but it's not. It's Roman.

So you spit back. You think you missed. Roman cackles. Both of you are on your knees, spitting and ducking. And laughing. It's dark and you can't see, even with adjusted eyes, but you can feel her spit in different spots and you think about her feeling your spit too. You're probably missing more than she is. Your aim sucks and you hit the wrong things.

Roman isn't the type of woman to read at the gym. She doesn't even go to the gym. She's the type of woman who pours salt in doorways and shoots at anything that comes close to the property line.

Roman's breathing has changed. She tumbles into you and falls on top of you, out of breath, laughing. Her hip bone digs into your thigh but you don't really mind.

"That was disgusting," you say.

You feel her smile. She says, "Nah."

You have never done anything like that with anyone before.

The two of you are still breathing heavy, but lying next to each other. You do that a lot lately.

She smooths her hair down but leaves her shirt folded up on her waist.

"You know, my dad's not exactly dad of the year either," Roman starts.

"Why? What'd he do?"

"He got drunk at my twelfth birthday party."

"That sucks, but –"

"Then hit on my friend's mom." While her own mom stood right there and watched. She said he probably forgot his god was watching too.

You let out a deep sigh.

Roman sighs too, almost in unison. She rests her head against your shoulder. You think a piece of your hair falls in her face. If it does, she doesn't move it.

"Men don't get it. They never will," she adds.

You've seen the way men look at Roman. Like she is all body. Like that one time she wore your too-small-for-you dress that she borrowed. The men whistled. But even how women have looked at her like she's a prize they'll never be. She's a trophy to everyone.

You want to change the subject. You tell Roman you've thought about dying your hair blonde. She says she hadn't even noticed it was brown. You don't tell her that she asked about your hair color the day you met.

She's lying on her side and, for someone who usually has a sort of slim, boxy figure, this position gives her some curves.

This makes you pay attention to your own body, its shape. You wonder if Roman notices any kind of curves on you. You wonder if you have curves, or if that is part of becoming a woman. You're still a girl, even if you don't like to think of yourself that way.

You think of what it means to be curvy – toes have curves. Ears have curves. You think about asking Roman if those things are sexy but decide not to. You instead ask yourself if those are sexy and you don't have an answer yet.

Roman's head turns a little. Her chin that was pressed against your shoulder is now softly in your collarbone. She's rolled halfway between her side and stomach, leaning on her elbows, so her chin moves up, next to your neck. You feel her breath, warm and sticky, as it falls on your skin.

You hold still as she makes all the moves around you. This is usually how it goes with Roman.

She says, "Let me help you with that," and with her right thumb, she softly rubs a spot on your chin. She's trying to remove some spit. The way she does it though is tender. It's more than just pointing out the corn someone has stuck between their teeth.

You feel your breath get caught in your throat a little. She notices. She lets go of one of her giggles and encourages you. Her mouth still next to your neck, she nearly kisses it.

No one's ever kissed your neck before.

The week you met Roman, you went to Dane's ranch-style house before school. You knew Dane from class although he never talked to you there. After all the hurrah the kids made when Luca invited you to the bleachers though, Dane said he felt bad. Said he was sure you were a good kisser. You wanted to be. He told you it would be a great start to a Monday morning.

You weren't sure why he asked you over before sunrise instead of after school, but you didn't ask. It became apparent that other people were happier telling you what to do than you knowing why.

You debated on going. What if this school year would just turn out to be a succession of boys inviting you to kiss them, until the end of the year, and still, no one wanted you.

You asked for his address and told him you'd meet him there. He told you that was great, but you'd need to make sure you left your shoes on the front porch, and be very quiet on your way in. No one else would know you were coming.

When you showed up, the sun was still tucked under the horizon, you couldn't see, and you put your shoes next to the doormat that said "The woods are my happy place." You weren't supposed to knock, so you just walked inside. Dane was sitting at the table, with his big, rounded shoulders, and pothole eyes. His brown hair looked like it should've been cut shorter but hadn't. He must have forgotten.

He placed his finger over his lips. Mouthed shhh. Wagged at you to follow him, so you two took tiny steps up the stairs to his bedroom. It might as well have been a small closet at the end of the hall.

At least the boy was there that time. Maybe it wasn't a joke.

"You can be very attractive," he said to you.

You took that as a compliment, although you weren't sure if that moment was one of those times or not.

He started lifting your shirt up over your arms. You wanted him to kiss you. You liked the way his dimples drew attention to his soft, plump cheeks. You wanted him to smile for you, but you'd never ask.

Then he said, "Shit."

A door down the hall squeaked open. Noisy, fumbly footsteps echoed down the stairs. He said, "Fuck." Then added, "Johnny's awake."

Dane had told you he normally woke up alone, drank a cup of leftover coffee from a day-old pot, and then left the house for school. His mom and stepdad slept through this routine. His mom stayed home on account of a disability, because of her mental health problems, and his stepdad didn't need to go to work until the sun was out.

Something made this day different.

Dane hoped his stepdad went down to lie on the couch and you could sneak out since the couch wasn't near the front. So you sat at the top of the stairs, ready to leave at any moment. He walked downstairs, then came right back up to tell you that no, Johnny's sitting at the kitchen table which was actually right next to the door.

You whispered, "Just tell him."

Dane said, "No way. After not even getting any?"

Finally Dane decided to ask Johnny to help him find his football uniform or something. He said he wasn't sure where he left it, and in the midst of them searching for something that wasn't lost, you snuck out the door. You never talked to him again.

You've told Roman that you've been naked with boys, but you weren't sure she believed you. She shouldn't, even if you did try and convince her.

Roman's mostly makeup-free, so she doesn't rub any off on you as she makes her climb. She's on top of you, kissing your neck in a way that's less sloppy than you imagined this kind of thing would be.

She doesn't go above the chin or below the collarbones. It's just your neck she's pressed against.

In your head you imagine wrapping your knobby fingers around her throat and choking her, but then nothing comes out. She doesn't even squeak. What good are imaginary friends for?

Roman's eyelashes seem to drift.

She says, "You have soft skin." She adds, "Pretend I'm one of the boys you like."

But you can't.

She grabs your hair and jerks your head back a little. Bigger surface area. More throat. She runs her tongue against it now. Nibbles it with her teeth. She's good.

She has to know this is your first time doing this, and she doesn't want you to forget it.

You manage to get out, "Roman," but she thinks it means you like it. And you think you do. But that's not what that meant. You're trying to ask her to stop. You think.

"Roman," you say again and she begrudgingly comes up for air.

"What?"

"Maybe no," you say.

"Maybe no." She repeats.

"I just think –"

"It's fine." She backs away.

But also maybe yes. You're not sure.

People have believed in themselves for hundreds of years. They must have. We like to believe that people have always behaved to some extent like modern humans, because it's hard to imagine anything different. Imagining people as behaving any differently would have to mean that we aren't right. The decisions we make aren't the only ones, if there were other ones before. Maybe they aren't true.

You've been in the dark long enough now that you're able to see her better. She's not wearing any makeup, but yours is smeared on her face. Not her lips, but her forehead, where she ran it into your mouth while she was taking care of the space underneath your jaw.

After some thought, "I like you," she says.

You still can't figure out how to breathe. Your stomach tightens up.

Changing the subject, "We can be even closer." She adds, "I want to be closer." She asks, "Do you? Because I have another idea."

And even if kissing Roman, the possibility of having sex with her, felt like suffocating or drowning or maybe both, you do still want to be closer. Even if you can't figure out why. You've decided that you like getting wet. Swimming in water feels exotic.

She says, "Cool. Good." (Turn to page 87.)

Roman tells you to go get some paper and something to write with.

You are going to make a list.

"A list?"

"Are you a broken record? Yes. A list. We're going to make a list, so get something you can write with."

Of all the things you two have done, of all the things you two could do, you're not sure how a list will make you closer.

But fine. What Roman wants, Roman gets, and she swears this will make you closer.

Other than Roman, there was only one other time someone stopped you to talk at a gas pump and it was Kia's mom and aunt. It was the end of winter and the start of spring. You hadn't talked to Kia in over six months.

It started quietly. You were pouring gas into your car when you heard your name from the other side of the pump.

You peered around it. They saw you looking, so the talking got louder. Intentionally.

"Hi, honey," Kia's mom said. Being sweet as if you'd seen each other at her Friday dinner last week, like you used to join when you were younger. You both knew you hadn't seen each other in months and it was all a charade.

"How's your mom?"

You lied.

"Your birthday just passed, didn't it? Happy birthday!"

Thank you.

Then her mom and aunt said you should not be wearing just a hoodie in this weather, you needed something warmer, so Kia's aunt came around the pump and put a scarf on your neck, and it was just kind of weird.

And then she said, "Are you feeling better?" And you said yes, because you were.

It was still a charade.

Roman says, "All right. Get going. Make a list of the prettiest girls you know. Put them in order, with prettiest at the top."

"Why?"

"I'll tell you after. Just do it."

"But what about you? Are you going to write one?"

She says, "I already know mine."

You've dreamt about Roman. She doesn't know. In your dream you and her are lying in your driveway, looking at the few stars you can see barely sprinkled in the sky. She tells you that you do exist. You blush, tell her she doesn't need to say that, but she taps you on the arm and says, "Yes! It's true!" and she stands up, with you still lying on the ground, and she shouts, "She exists! She exists!"

You can't really see any of the stars in the sky anymore.

You think through the girls you might put on this list. You already told Roman that Kia would be at the top, but just because you said that, you're not so sure.

You're also thinking about what makes some the "est." Pretty-est. Because there are some girls who are gorgeous – almond-shaped eyes, heart-shaped lips, and wispy, weedy bodies – but they have different noses, so which one is prettier?

This list is harder than it seems.

You've started writing names down but in no order. Right now they're just one conglomerate of girls who are prettier than you.

Roman looks over your shoulder.

"That's not really a list."

"I'm working on it," you say.

She rocks her head and mocks you, silently saying, *I'm working on it*. She says, "Is it really that hard? Don't you already know these names?"

You thought you did, but maybe you don't.

You don't feel like you exist when you look at the names on this paper.

Roman had told you her birthday is in August. At that point, you'd spent enough time together that you felt like you should get her a gift. You woke up at three in the afternoon on a Saturday and went by yourself to the mall. You thought hard about what to get her. Whether it should be something she'd like, or something you wanted her to like.

You ended up at the junk shop in the corner of the first floor. An unusual store some Joe Shmo turned into a resale shop between a JCPenny and Claire's. He had umbrella stands, porch geese, and mason jars. Near the register was a cardboard box of photographs. School portraits, family vacations, and babies' first steps. After filing through them for twenty minutes, you bought three. Each at least sixty years old, and of three different little girls. In all the photos, the girls were alone, wearing dresses and Mary Janes. One girl had a scar on her face, a deep line from her left eye to the top of her lip. You could see this, because the girl, behind a car, was looking over her shoulder. On the back of the photo, in wobbly writing, it said, *hide and seek*. The man at the register didn't even ask why you were buying them. He must be used to people keeping memories of girls.

You gave Roman the photos for her birthday that evening. You thought they were funny or eerie in the way that thinking about people who never knew you existed is. Like maybe you'd be giving Roman more than just pictures as a gift.

But you said, or did, something wrong. Like, you had to have. You said happy birthday, and she nodded her head like she was listening, but who wants to listen to that shit when they're handed pictures of strange little girls who are probably dead. Like now it's her job to keep them alive, and she never even knew them.

She immediately set them on the table after opening the recycled cardboard necklace box you put them in and now you're sure you screwed things up because you saw them in the trash later after she yawned and told you it was time to leave. Had different plans for her birthday that night.

You had also gone to Bath and Body Works that afternoon to get yourself lotion since you were out. After looking for quite some time, the stout woman with too much blush at the register told you it was discontinued. She asked if she could help you find something new to love.

It was the only lotion you liked, so you knew your skin would soon get dry.

You finish. It's hard, and might not all be the truth, but who the hell cares. Roman doesn't know who any of these people are anyway.

"So why'd you have me do this?" You ask again.

"When you made this list, you compared yourself, didn't you?"

You think *duh*, but just say, "A little."

"I want you to realize this list means nothing. Every girl wants to be on a list like this. Thousands, maybe millions, of these lists exist in the world, and most of the girls on those lists aren't on yours. Right?"

"I don't know them."

She shushes you with her hand. At first she waves it around, then she almost covers your mouth with it but stops herself. You would have let her.

"The point is, those lists mean nothing. They aren't the truth." She rests her hand on your leg. "Besides, you probably know some of them. Now give me your list."

You hold the lined piece of notebook paper tightly to your chest. It's covering your heart.

"Why?"

She pulls a pink lighter out of her back pocket and ignites it. The flame flickers at first, then holds itself steady. She holds it out to you. "We're going to burn it." A soft glow hovers in just the immediate space around it. Threatening.

"C'mon. Give me your list. We're going to burn it."

She's holding her other hand open, ready to take the paper from you, but you're not willing to give it up. You notice the lines on her palm that might mean something.

You move past her hand and stick the paper directly in the fire. No one needs to know who is on it.

Besides, you're pretty sure she just wants to see where she falls on the list. Because that's what all the girls want. Just like she says.

You didn't even put Roman on it.

Roman once introduced you to Crystal. They weren't friends exactly, but the girl gave Roman something to anticipate. Roman told you that Crystal could tell you your future. Said something about how she told Crystal and her mom that she'd bring you to meet them next time she saw them because she knew you needed hope.

Roman met Crystal at a bar on one of those mile roads where she was playing her guitar one night. Crystal didn't sing, just played the instrument. She wore a dress with a fake leather bodice and flowy half skirt. It had tiny purple flowers printed on it. She had the perfect mouth for singing, even if she couldn't actually sing, and she had rough fingers because of her guitar.

So Roman took you, or you took Roman, to the back of the bar, so you could meet Crystal and her mom. She had just finished her set.

The two women sat at a wooden picnic table out back. Crystal was sweaty and didn't try to hide it. Her mom wore a regular red t-shirt, probably from Kmart, and a pair of faded mom jeans. She didn't have a wedding band, but did wear reading glasses.

Crystal read your palm. She held your hand, her tough fingers pressing into it, and she looked at all of the marks on your skin like you never had before. You had looked at your body, many, many times, in fact, but never in this way. She was seeing something on you that you never had.

Her mom was there to watch over her. It seems that if you are telling a woman her future, you need supervision.

Crystal held your hand, read your energy, and told you, "You will suffer."

You already knew that.

Not putting Roman on your list was a lie.

Girls will always keep secrets. It's the only thing they will have.

Roman says, "Well, didn't burning that list feel good?" although her tone is less than enthusiastic.

You shrug.

"Okay, how about this. Think about those girls. What do they have that you don't?"

Everything. The answer is everything. But you say, "They're beautiful."

"How? And are they really? Or do they have confidence?"

They have round eyes without craters below. Milk-smooth skin. Small noses. Frail bodies. Hands without grabs. And yeah, they must have confidence.

You don't have to respond. Roman says, "Fake it 'til you make it."

"How?"

This might be one of those times that you're supposed to answer the question yourself, but you don't know how.

"Get yourself dressed in something that makes you feel good and let's go show you off."

You roll your eyes, but Roman's patting her hand on your leg. This must be how house pets feel, getting rubbed. It feels nice. You understand the need for attention and consider begging for it from now on like a cat.

She says, "If you're acknowledged, you exist. Let's get you existing."

Roman repeats herself. If you want to be like the girls you yourself wrote down on that list – the girls you're jealous of – she says, "There's a party tomorrow night downtown. I'll give you the address. Get dressed up and come." You could agree to go, to see what Roman means (turn to page 37), or, she wouldn't be thrilled about it, but she says if you don't want to do that, she has another idea. It'll just be you two (turn to page 28).

But you're still thinking about how apparently it turns out you haven't existed up until this point.

With your left hand flat on your nightstand, you paint your nails red with the polish you stole from the side pocket of a girl's backpack in fourth hour. The way your nails are shaped makes them look like wide upper teeth. If the teeth were completely soaked in blood.

You hope Jessica will take your picture with her camera when you're finished. You've been straightening your hair with a round brush and blow dryer, blackening your lower eye with melted kohl, and making your lips the perfect shape with a red lipstick your mother no longer wears. You've gotten good at it. Looking like this seems like something you'll never want to forget, which is why you plan to hang out with Jessica.

She wants to get together sometime soon anyway. She met a new boy who does not like her holding onto photos of her ex. She says she must burn them and she wants to turn it into a party. You're not sure who else might be there, but she invited you. It feels like something you should show up to.

You look at the magazine cutouts taped to your wall. They have overtaken the space and now completely cover the photos of you and Kia. They are pictures of strange, beautiful women in uncomfortable poses and with mouths open so wide people think they are smiling. Your mother hasn't asked why you've hung these up. She must know.

You finish the nails on your left hand and while they look perfect, you realize too late that it would have been smarter to start with your non-dominant hand. You always ruin your painted nails when you try to hold the brush. You know you have to accept that your right hand is fucked before you even get to it.

"All right. Let's find a screwdriver," she tells you as she pulls her lighter out. You see the fluid in it swish back and forth.

"For what?"

She smiles. She pats your arm like a puppy dog would if it could and pulls it toward her. Runs her spiny finger up and down your triceps. "This space on your arm here looks so plain." She says. She emphasizes, "PLAIN."

"Thanks. It's an arm." What is it supposed to look like?

She rolls her eyes at you but the way her lashes move makes it look more like a dance.

"Let's dress it up." She continues to rub the spot she's talking about with her thumb. It feels tender.

While she's doing this, she tells you all about branding, how much of a high you get from it, "And I would know a little something about highs," she adds. Winks. You imagine her digging a screwdriver through your flesh. Is this how Jesus felt before his execution?

She tells you that it shows a bond. A very important bond. You two can be sisters. She tells you how you'll be connected, but also be different at the same time. Best of two worlds.

"Most people don't have these." She lifts her arm to show her own scar built up in the same spot she poked on you.

It's a plump patch of smooth, red tissue that was damaged once. Some kind of spotty heart the size of a dime that was done haphazardly. One side is smaller than the other.

She adds, "Let's make you exist."

"What if I don't want to exist?"

"I want you to."

You remember a time outside the dollar store on Maple Road. The windows were smudged but big, making it easy to see both in and out. The window was like a divider between two worlds, even though both sides were still visible to the other.

You'd never been in there before.

Roman asked to stop there, needed to go in, so you dropped her off. Parked the car across from the front door. You watched Roman walk across the lot, on her way inside. A man who passed her on his way out turned to catch her one last time behind him and made a cat-call. When the door shut behind her, you could almost see your reflection.

"People suck," she says.

You can't argue with her.

She rolls the lighter around her palm and tells you that one day, you will be a whole different person. Someone you can't even know now. Because of this, you should do whatever you want. One day, these choices you have will be gone. "And, to be honest," she adds, "you won't even remember them. Especially if you don't make them."

You cross your legs on top of hers with your butt pressed against her thigh. You can see her belly button ring through the thin fabric of her tank. Roman's like a cartoon character, practically wears the same outfit every day.

She breathes like she's about to say something, but then she holds it.

You say, "What?" Even though you know this is probably a bad idea because, for a split second, you think about how the things she says can feel like target practice with knives.

She asks what you masturbate with. This comes out of nowhere.

Hands. You could just say your hands, but that would be a lie.

First, "Why do you ask?"

She shrugs. She always has an answer to everything until she doesn't want to.

She says, "Sometimes I use highlighters." You wonder if that's true, or if it's bait. Then you can't feel your fingers as your own answer comes to mind. You can't feel your breath. Can't feel your words. You think you bit one in half and then taste its juice. You might die if you say it. That's what it feels like, anyway. You'd rather eat fermented words.

Roman's looking at you. Wide eyes like a cat's. Curious and attentive. She's waiting.

You shake your head. Sink as far into your spine as you can.

"Come on."

You twist. You've never told anyone this.

She laces her fingers between yours. "Just tell me."

You're trying to decide if it's meant to feel – you stop thinking about it. You say, "Sometimes I use my electric toothbrush." You almost choke on your own breath.

"Liar. You don't have an electric toothbrush!" She practically shouts. She adds, "I've been in your bathroom before. It's just those blue and green plastic ones from the drugstore."

Why did she notice that?

You admit that the one you use is one you'd gotten yourself. Your mother wouldn't have bought that for you. She says why'd you get it. You tell her you read about it in a sex magazine. She says so. You had wondered what it might feel like and wanted to try it. You don't keep it in the bathroom. You almost die when you tell her this.

She scrunches her nose at you. Rolls her eyes. Pulls your body in closer and rubs her fingers through your hair. You feel a fingernail get caught and she uncatches it, pulls it, like it isn't attached to you.

"It's fine. I'm teasing you."

Roman's the type of girl who'd have circled her photo in your yearbook and written "Hi! Ur friend" next to it. The type of girl you'd only have talked to for a few months, but never forgotten about.

You notice the paper square sticking out of Roman's pocket, so you change the subject.

"What's with the funeral card?" You've seen her with it before. The face of some old man above a Bible quote. She ignores your question. "I know you carry it with you."

Roman tilts her head and looks at you with unamused bedroom eyes.

You think about how she's ruthless when she asks you questions. "Go on. Tell me," you say. You might try being more like her.

"It's for my grandfather."

This is the first time you're hearing of him. You go to ask what happened, but Roman continues on her own. She says, "I guess sometimes we like to hold onto the things we never had."

She picks a single strand of hair off her shoulder. You're unsure if it's yours or hers. Then, unsolicited, "He left when my ma was a baby."

You say oh. Shit.

Roman sits up and adjusts her spine. She looks like the taut chain of a fancy chandelier. You've never had a fancy chandelier so you don't know what to do with it.

You ask what happened. She says nothing. You tell her you know that's not true. Fine, she says.

She tells you she was a waitress when she was younger, and you think, what, seventeen or something? And she says an old man came in. The hostess sat him in her section. So she served him. Brought him his Angus beef burger he ordered, dropped off his ale, and then gave him his bill. You wonder how she remembers details like that.

"Told him it was nice meeting him." Still straight, not touching you, Roman looks like she knows what she's talking about. As always. "Then he stopped me, grabbed my arm, and although I didn't have time to be fightin' an old man at work, I almost punched him. He told me I had familiar eyes. Sounded like a bad pickup line. Gross, dude. I'm not interested."

He asked her why, like she knew the answer. Then he asked her if she knew a Tom.

"Told him no, but then I thought about it. I told him 'I guess you could call it that.' Never met him, but I know that's my ma's dad's name." She sighs. "My customer told me that Tom was his brother."

You are working on persistence when you tell her, more like ask her, to say what happened next. Persistence is challenging.

"I asked how Tom was doing and the guy told me he died a few years back." She cracks her knuckles so loud you hurt. "I told him that Tom was my grandfather I'd never met."

You crack your knuckles too.

"He left Grandma when my ma was born."

You think, men are like that sometimes. Distant.

You ask again about the funeral card. Why she carries it. She pulls it out of her pocket and folds it between her fingers like she's performing a magic trick. You almost expect it to disappear. She tells you that Grandpa Tom died from cancer. The customer, Martin, told her that before he died, the family asked Tom if he wanted them to find her ma for him. He said no.

Roman takes a breath. You watch her lips make a small void as they open and close. She says, "Martin got up and left without paying his bill. I was livid." After a pause, she adds, "Then he came back to give me my cash, and an envelope of Tom's stuff to take, because there had been no one else to take it."

You say nothing because you are irresponsible.

"The only thing that seemed important from it was his obituary. It listed no kids."

She puts her hands down behind her so she's leaning back, her opened chest facing you. You notice her collarbones. They look like little mountains drawn below her neck.

"Did I ever tell you that I almost died once?" She asks this casually as she starts tapping her feet. Luckily the tapping is too soft for it to bother you.

You say, what? No.

"Yeah. When I was ten. I swam under a plastic pool cover and almost stopped breathing. Couldn't escape."

You think about how swimming just isn't any good.

"I'm glad you didn't die," you say.

She nudges your shoulder playfully. Her hand feels cold. She pushes your feet aside, rolls on her stomach, and stretches herself into a Superman pose. She turns her neck over her shoulder so she's looking back at you and says, "How about you? Have you almost died?"

No, you don't think so.

She rolls her eyes. "Have you at least thought about when you'll die?"

You don't answer.

She says, "I bet you don't even think you're going to die."

"That's not true. I mean, I know I will. Everyone does."

She ignores you and continues, "You wanna know why no one thinks they're going to die?" She doesn't wait for an answer. "No one thinks they're going to die because death looks different for everyone. You can't imagine it." She takes a deep inhale. "They always talk about representation in media or some shit, they say it's important, because 'if you can believe it, you can be it'. If you see someone looking like you out there saving the animals, or running the country, you suddenly think you can do it too. You realize it's a possibility. But with death, even though someone who looks just like you has died before, for some reason, you still can't imagine it." She exhales. She says, "I guess it's because we won't look at those people when they die. We don't wanna look death in the face."

You don't remember what the man in the dollar store parking lot, the one calling back to Roman, looked like. You try picturing his face but the most you can imagine is his frame. The outline of some big object you can't identify. You figure it must not matter.

"But you're not dead yet. This is your time to live."

"You know, you really talk a lot." This is the first time you have said something you mean to be offensive.

She ignores you. "Do you want to be the prettiest girl you know?"

What does that even mean?

"Because now's your time to do it. What if you died tomorrow?" But she ignores you again. "All I'm saying is: there are ways to get noticed. What if I can help you get noticed?"

"How?"

You are a congregation at the foot of a sermon.

You realize you're making it all up. The dollar store trip was never real. You are sure you only imagined Roman in that parking lot, walking across the blacktop, entering the dollar store.

It never happened.

Roman likes to listen to a singer who can't play her own instrument, but has a band full of women behind her. Women who are probably lesbians. You watched their music video on television and couldn't help but fall in love. You're still trying to decide if it was with the song or the women on stage.

She starts waving the funeral card around. She says, "I told you. Having kids is selfish." Then using her second hand to grab it, she rips the cardstock in half, right down the center of his face. Suddenly it doesn't mean anything to her, but you remind yourself that nothing's real. It's like he never existed.

Women are like that too sometimes.

"So do you want that brand or what?" She's pressing her fingers against your soft, pulpy flesh again.

You ask her what happens if you say no, and she tells you that would be silly. "Seriously, it will mean something. It's like an initiation."

Into what?

"What if I get in trouble?" Then you add, "It's like a tattoo." Then you ask yourself who'd punish you.

"It's less noticeable. It blends in." Her smile is sharp, like the light that floods from the crack of an open door. "And you can tell people it was an accident. Most scars are."

"It doesn't sound safe."

"You just have to take care of it." She points to her arm again. "I've done it before and I'm fine."

Occasionally Roman cleans your house.

If she is over in your room with you, she'll start straightening up. T-shirts, jewelry, pencils, makeup brushes, underwear. They are all just things to be put somewhere else. She doesn't even make a big deal of it. Doesn't tell you your room is dirty, or ask if you need help, or say she is doing it. She just starts and doesn't stop until it is finished and then your room always ends up looking better than it did by the time she leaves.

You think about how cleaning a house requires one to have a home.

You can't decide if that's a privilege or not.

A part of you trusts her, or maybe a part of you wants to trust her. And it would be different. And it would match her. Maybe people would notice you. You could exist. You could say yes (turn to page 97). But you think about your life before Roman, and after Roman, and consider saying no (turn to page 128).

In a dream you've had, Roman showed you how she took you. In real life, she doesn't know about this.

Occasionally she calls you names: honey, sweetheart, bitch. Right now, she's calling you pussy because you can't breathe through your nose. You're swallowing golf-ball-sized air and she hasn't even started yet.

"Will you just sit still? Nothing is touching you."

But it's going to, and knowing that is even worse.

She presses her fingers to her forehead and breathes deeply. "Do this with me," she says. "*Breathe*. In: one, two, three. Out: four, five, six. *Breathe*." You're not listening to her.

Roman told you before that one day you'd come face to face with your god. Everyone will.

Then she asked, "Who is your god? Is it your parents? Is it you?"

Roman said, "My god," but never finished her sentence.

Her telling you what to do right now doesn't make her God. You know this because God doesn't tell us what to do. He sits the whole thing out. Miracles are bullshit. This might make her a witness instead.

Roman's got you lying on your back so you won't pass out. She said it's supposed to keep your blood flowing or something. She's rubbing your head and all you can think about is how you haven't brushed your hair all day and it's a rat's nest. She's probably laughing at you.

She starts singing a throaty lullaby and you're not sure where she learned it from.

"Hush, little baby, don't say a word. Mama's gonna buy you a mockingbird."

Your mother used to sing lullabies to you, when you were a baby. Your earliest memory is of her. You on lap. Her hand on your back. Lips to forehead. Singing into your skin. You're in a dark room filled with shadows. Somewhere you have trouble identifying.

Roman's stopped petting your head and has started to dust the part of your arm she's trying to brand with her fingers. It feels like a soft kiss.

"This will show you how tough you are," she says to you.

"What if I'm not tough?"

"Don't think like that." She says this as a serious statement.

You breathe deep. You breathe wide. You fill with warm air.

When you were young, you dared Terry to an arm wrestle. You told him you could take him and win, so he called you a liar and said sure. Asked some of the kids on the playground to come watch so you couldn't spread rumors after. You ended up with an audience of three. Ragboy Ryan who reminded everyone of Pig-Pen from Peanuts, Cocky Cole who got his name in high school after you all learned the word cocky, and little Janey. Terry had you on the jungle gym set, sitting in wood chips next to some slide steps to rest your elbows on. He asked one of the boys to whistle when it was time to start, and because Ragboy Ryan couldn't whistle, it was up to Cocky Cole. You could see Terry mouth a countdown anyway, but then the whistle went and you pushed with all your might.

Terry was a fighter and he wanted to play dirty. He tried pinching the skin on your hand with his fingers as he clamped down. He almost licked his nose with his tongue. Trying to make you laugh? (You learned later in life that boys sometimes combine pain and humor. Maybe some weird coping mechanism that leaves girls suffering.) But it was the color that looked like a birthmark in his eye that almost got you. It was a small speck of gold in a sea of cobalt blue that was a distraction. It didn't distract you enough though. (Maybe girls suffering is how boys win.)

Cocky Cole called champion with another whistle, and you won with a woodchip stuck in your hair.

Terry told the kids to forget about telling everyone about the fight. Said you were a liar and a cheater and he doesn't play with cheaters.

Roman doesn't know this story.

"Look. Just think about how cool you'll be now when you go to parties."

That would be nice, you think. You say sure. You don't know anyone with a brand.

"Other than me," she reminds you.

"Right." Can't forget.

"Is there something I'm supposed to do to care for this?"
You ask.

"Yeah, but it's not hard." She's started whispering.

"And this will be permanent?"

"Usually."

You elbow yourself up. "What does that mean?"

"*Shh*. Stop asking questions."

Roman puts her hand over your mouth. You can't pin it, but you taste some sort of leftover drug she must have held. Some sweat. The skin of a sinner. Or a witness. Maybe both.

"I promise. You're going to be so cool," she says to you.

Kia invited you to a party during your freshman year. Neither of you knew the girl hosting it. Kia just found a flyer stuck to the bathroom floor at school and said you guys could be cool if you went.

The two of you got ready for it together. She was in a black crop top that had mesh midriff with the word BRAT in silver sequins across the chest. She had on a black pleather miniskirt and fishnet stockings. There's no way her mom bought that outfit for her. Her mom had tight brown curls and pink turtleneck sweaters.

Kia couldn't decide between a pair of combat boots or ballet flats. Edgy or poised?

You put on a velvet dress that was down to your ankles, faded in the center from some old, washed-out stain. You got it at a thrift store, so who knows what had happened to it in its former life.

At school "the girls" don't talk to you unless they want something. At school "the girls" don't want something unless it involves a boy with a tattoo or vodka. This means you're alone.

One of those days, Catalogue Carly invites you to the city fair later. She says she's trying to get a group to go. It will be fun. Can you imagine the laughs on the tilt-a-whirl or what. Haha. She blows a bubble with the gum in her mouth and smears a little bit of her lip gloss. She's in a black turtleneck t-shirt with a layered yellow dress. She looks like she belongs in a JCPenny advertisement. You've never talked before and she's one of "the girls." You would say no except you want to go to the fair anyway, and you're sure there will be vodka.

You also haven't heard from Roman in two weeks.

That night, you walk past a dried worm on the concrete, a string of Christmas lights in front of the fair, and the woman with a bowl cut selling tickets in a little booth. "Hey," she calls after you. "Hey. You can't go in there without tickets. No rides," she yells.

You tell her you don't plan to ride anything anyway.

You see Catalogue Carly and Second-Base Sheridan and Lipstick Lisa holding water bottles that you know don't have any water. They are all standing in front of a row of porta potties. Carly and Sheridan are in sundresses. Carly has white sunglasses shaped like hearts. Lisa usually wears sweatshirts and leggings - this is the first time you think you've seen her in shorts. She looks cute and you almost feel like you want to be here.

"Here," Sheridan says. This might be the first thing she's said to you since fourth grade when she said your pigtails were stupid. She hands you a water bottle and winks. Her wink is uncomfortable.

"Drink up," Carly adds. She takes a sip. She blows in Sheridan's face as if trying to prove she's a delinquent. Sheridan laughs and hiccups. Lisa laughs louder.

You hear a hollow banging come from behind the girls. A couple in their twenties fall out of a porta potty door that swings open, the woman hanging off the man's shoulders. The two people laugh. The man has strawberry blonde hair and the woman's is straight red. She has thick black wings around her brown eyes. The man's hands are big as if they hold a football. The couple would look like they belong in a movie if they weren't falling out of a portable toilet.

"That's going to be you in a minute," Carly says to you.

"Excuse me?" You haven't even taken a sip of what you assume is vodka yet. You take a drink and notice that it's watered down.

"Yeah. Wait a second-" Carly waves her hand. Someone's behind you. You take another sip and turn to see Carter. He's your height and a little overweight. You've never even thought twice about him. That's because he's not a complete wreck like some kids at school, but he's also nothing special.

"You ready, Carter?" Lisa caws. He looks at you, smiles sheepishly, and shrugs his shoulders. It's almost like he's saying to you *let's do this.*

It looks like everyone is in on the joke.

"What? What is this?"

"Get in there," Sheridan says. Carter ducks his head as he steps up and into the plastic tower. You shake yours.

"Come on. You have to."

On your way to school that morning you passed a car with the license plate: B4RK4M3.

You barked. You opened your mouth wide and a guttural noise from the back of your throat escaped. Over and over until you stopped. It was a sound you didn't recognize as your own.

The driver didn't even know. He never would. What's the point?

Carter's sitting on the toilet which is just a deep hole in a bench. He tries to pull you onto his lap but you shake your head.

"Just real quick," he says.

The place smells like a rotting animal. Carter's starting to plug his nose. He's grabbed your back and tries pulling you in. You're shaking your head, eyes closed, and you trip. Knee him in the crotch. He moans but catches your lips with his on your fall. You hear some "*oohs*" come from outside. You almost spit in the boy's face. You turn to open the door and fall out. You hear a snap.

"The girls" are holding a Polaroid camera. Laughing. They pull an instant photo from the machine. One of them hides it between the skin of her stomach and the fabric of her shirt so it stays dark.

"You're welcome!" They call after you as you start running in the other direction. "Just wanted to help you finally get that kiss!"

"And record it too!" Another one yells out.

You know the photo is for instant proof. Their laughter isn't enough.

"Scrapbook it!"

You realize you left the shitty vodka in the plastic poop box with Carter. Why couldn't you be as happy as that other couple that came falling out?

You come inside from tanning. Spent all afternoon in the backyard dripping in butter and iodine. You sat on rows of foil paper. You were trying to burn. Kia told you that if you burn three times you tan better, so she taught you all these tricks.

"Where've you been?" Your mother asks as you throw the leftover tinfoil in the top kitchen drawer.

Outside.

"Doing what?"

You look at her.

"Answer me."

Nothing.

"Looks like you've been tanning."

Maybe. Your hair is tied up in a knot and you're wearing cut-off shorts and a bra.

"You shouldn't do that."

You say to her that she shouldn't tell you what to do. You know that she used to tan like this.

"I'm looking out for you," she nearly yells as you walk past her. She tells you to stop and come back.

No thanks. You're going to church. You put your tennis shoes on and start tying them.

Your mother isn't finished. She stands above you and says, "You're tryin' real hard to look like something you're not." She talks about how boys want more than tans. They want blah blah seasoned girls blah who are blah blah blah and skin.

Boys watch girls who do this kind of stuff, she looks your oiled body up and down, and those girls get passed around. You start humming so you can't hear her, but still, you hear her say, "You know, if you keep acting like this, you'll only be good for one thing" anyway. You'd be a good girl for boys to practice on.

You show her your middle finger and walk out the door. She doesn't bring it up again.

It has been days since you've last heard from Roman. You've stopped going home after school and instead end up in the West House boys' bathroom.

In eighth grade, you promised you wouldn't tell anyone when Sam Jenkins told you and Kia that almost any girl could get sex if she wanted in high school if she went to the West House bathroom. You never did tell anyone, but now you're in tenth grade and looking at Gus Porter who was just hanging around the sinks when you walked inside. He's known to paint his nails green and has hair down to his shoulders.

You are second-guessing everything.

You told him you would have sex but only if you went somewhere else to do it, and if by sex you guys could agree on a blow job instead. That sounded like a good place to start. You didn't tell Gus that you'd never had sex before and you didn't want him to see your bra since it's from the thrift store. It's stained brown. He asked if you deep throat good. You told him yes and he asked why he doesn't know you then.

As you two left the bathroom, you watched Melissa Arlington and Kyle Ingram walk past you. Kyle had a big, round, red spot on his neck. You think it was lipstick.

When Gus sees you pass him in lunch the next day, you overhear him tell his friends you're a baby. You hear him say that all you'd give him was a blow job but then you wouldn't even do that because someone was watching. Pussy. He doesn't tell them that you were on the top of an elementary school slide and the people who would have been watching were a mother and son. You didn't want to give him a blow job anyway.

Friday is a half day. You go to the church and take a bottle of wine for yourself. For a place that's meant to represent a body of believers, no body is ever there. You think something about how maybe that's the way bodies work, but aren't sure of the meaning. You take the bottle to the gas station and drink until it is empty behind the dumpster. It smells, but you are so drunk you don't even notice. You watch a woman holding a Harlequin romance novel leave the station and go back to her car.

You still haven't talked to Roman and it has been a few weeks. You aren't sure where she is.

When Roman finally returns after another week, she says, "You know, I might destroy you," and you can't tell if that is supposed to be a promise or a threat or something more. You hope for more.

She wanted to come over to give you that brand she talked about before. Showed up at your place unannounced when her dealer dropped her off.

She doesn't knock on your door. Just walks in and publicizes her presence by loudly singing a song she is unsure the words of.

When you come out of your room, you see her in her same stained boyfriend pants but a new top. It is a thin, loose, gray t-shirt with blue horizontal stripes. She has a black tattoo choker necklace on but you're not sure where she got it from.

You want to hug her fiercely.

Roman asks if you changed your sheets as she brushes you in the hallway. Her hanging hand hard against you as she slinks past.

You've never told her that you typically don't change your sheets. This is a ritual for her when she arrives and you aren't sure why. Ripping them off the bed and throwing them in the washer with nothing else.

Then the two of you are sitting in your bathroom, your shirtless back against the bubblegum-pink, one-inch tiles that make the walls. The house was built in the mid-twentieth century. This is the first time you sit half-naked with anyone and you're grateful your mother isn't home. Roman said it would make the branding easier if there was nothing in the way. You hope she's right. That this is easy.

"Where's your mom?"

She is still dressed but has pulled the end of her shirt up and back down through itself so it hugs her chest like some kind of cross between a crop top and bra. You used to fix your shirts like that when you were younger and danced on your bed, lip-syncing to Britney Spears and Christina Aguilera's top hits. You pretended you were a sexy woman.

What you mean is you pretended you were someone people would remember.

"Work." She could be there, anyway.

"She's never home. Will you introduce me one day?"

"I don't think so."

Roman doesn't challenge you. She knows what it's like to be on her own. There's not much to show.

Roman has a working lighter this time. Said it is brand new and the pressure is fantastic. It will heat the screwdriver up no problem.

"Is a dinky little lighter like that going to be hot enough?"

"Sure." She says it like you are simply incapable of understanding. "Do you want me to heat it up longer? Because I can." What you don't know is that she's thinking about how the chance of infection gets higher if it's hotter.

You regret asking. You put your hand on her thigh.

"Trust me," she says.

You want to trust her but aren't sure you can. You hold onto her thigh harder.

She doesn't ask if you are ready, but she has the screwdriver sitting in the flame because she is ready.

You are wondering if you should ask Roman where she's been the last few weeks when she says, "You ever wanted to see the worst of humanity?" You squint your eyes in a way that you think obviously says no, but Roman keeps talking. She wasn't actually asking you that question.

"Take a drive (downtown) during rush hour. People will cut each other's throats."

Then suddenly the backside of your arm feels like it has split open. Your initial instinct is to pull away, but Roman has a death grip on you, to hold you down.

The burning screwdriver unzips a small part of your arm apart with healing being the only option to zip it back up. You still wriggle.

"Stop moving," Roman commands, leaning over you. "We're only halfway there."

She digs the screwdriver back in and drags another short line.

Years ago you started finding yourself in strange places. Unsure of how you got there. Had never been there. Like someone invited you outside yourself then borrowed your body for a while. They put on glossy eyes and mannequin limbs. A face taken from a poem. You had no say in the matter, but the costume fit you nicely. Your mother ignored this. Didn't ask you who you were or where you went. Didn't say she knew you were missing.

She picked you up from your uncle's. You said nothing. Nothing. There was silence. Then finally she said what's wrong. Nothing. At home, she sat you down at the kitchen table where there was a salt shaker, no pepper, and she said that sometimes people are ghosts, gone, off. They feel like they are viewing things from outside their body. There is a name for it. She got up and left.

She said people. You didn't know boys did it, but you knew some of your girlfriends did – and never by choice. Some of them soundless when other kids yelled. Some of them robots when they were called names. Even still, other girls stepped outside themselves when they dressed (in ways that would make people look).

You had thought it was all just a part of being a girl.

"It's done," she says, pulling the weapon away. You see the two of you, sweating next to a toilet surrounded by candy pink. She starts rubbing your forehead. "You'll be fine."

You don't say anything. Just stare at the dusty ceiling. No one in this house dusts.

You remember that your tits are still out as she wipes her newly-moist palm on the side of her pants and pulls her shirt down from its makeshift shape.

You wonder whose brand hers matches.

When you and Kia were fourteen and freshmen, you two obsessed over boys.

Kia couldn't get enough of Kenny, some knobby-kneed baseball player who was emotionally unavailable but had a nice hair swoop in the front. You, on the other hand, were obsessed with Jordan, a drummer in the school band and just tall enough to be taller than you but in a good place to kiss. His lips reminded you of licorice. You wanted to taste them. In your mind, Jordan was the better option. It didn't matter though. As much as they were respectively yours in both of your heads – you both wrote them secret letters you never sent, listed their names on pages in your notebooks, and doodled pictures of them that you taped to your mirrors – it was never going to happen for either of you. Kenny had never even talked to Kia, and Jordan had told Kia that you were very "bizarre." You still had hope that what he said was a strange compliment. At least he paid attention to you.

Then you couldn't find Kia on the night of the spring formal where you were wearing that velvet thrift store dress that was faded on the front. You two had come together, then she went to get something to drink and didn't come back. Daughtry's "It's Not Over" started playing and that was one of Kia's favorite songs. You were certain she'd join you back on the dance floor for it, so you started dancing in preparation. Your arms were too long for your body at that age and they swung at your sides, back and forth. You put one foot in front, then one foot in back. Your eyes closed.

You felt a hand on your shoulder and you opened your eyes, grinning. The DJ's disco lights flashed across Nemo's face, the lamest kid in school, two grades below you. The laces on his dress shoes were pink and he wore a bow tie.

Kia hadn't come back. You stormed across the dance floor, in tears before even making it to the bathroom. Next to the bathroom door was Jordan slobbering all over Kia who was pushed up against a wall.

You two did not ride home together.

You stormed out of the school's gymnasium and don't know if they even heard you crying when you left them. You put a quarter in the payphone at the front of the school and rang your mother. You put in another quarter and you rang her again. You pressed the buttons harder the third time with the last quarter you had. She never answered.

You sat on the curb outside until your mother eventually picked you up. Twenty minutes past the agreed-upon time.

"Where's Kia?" She asked.

"She got a different ride."

You slammed the door shut. You locked it instinctively. You watched some girls with hair that was curled, then sweaty, walk down the street. Then a boy holding a girl around her shoulders while waiting.

There was a van stopped next to you at a red light with a ladder fastened to its roof. The light turned green. You went. There was a fire alarm sitting next to someone's trash bag left at the edge of their yard. You'd never want to live in a house on a main road. There was a boy with a nose ring riding a skateboard under street lamps. It was late. You cut your eyelashes off as a young child. Your mother smelt like apricots.

You weren't even sure if Jordan was kissing Kia's mouth. It looked like he was missing.

You couldn't help but wish he was missing on you.

You were at a red light again and suddenly couldn't breathe. Your mother pressed the gas when it finally turned green. She didn't ask how the dance was before you rushed inside and headed straight to your bedroom.

The next year, Jordan will be in your formal dance photos that Kia's parents will take, but it's because Kia is his date that time. This is after she dates both him and Kenny at the same time for a few months. She will eventually break up with Kenny because the boys don't like her dating both of them when they find out.

You wonder if these things that Kia did were why you let it 'slip' that Kia's dad was a registered sex offender when you were drinking with those other girls. Maybe it wasn't because you were drunk.

It probably doesn't matter why you told her secret.

It's been a week since the brand. Roman told you this tiny little burn would be fine and for some reason you trusted her. The burn is not fine though and it's gotten infected. Now your X-marks-the-spot is surrounded by a tender, red ring and has started pussing. When you lift your arm to inspect it, you realize that it has started to smell funny too.

Still, when she called you, begging you to pick her up from her sugar daddy's house, you couldn't say no. So now the two of you are sitting on a half-wall made of bricks that surrounds that church she sometimes stays at. You did not tell her that the wound's infected, but she also didn't ask.

Her fingers sliver through the long fur of a brown and gold stray cat that has wandered up to her. The fur is a little matted, so you notice that her fingers get caught sometimes, but she does her best to work through it.

"Can I tell you a secret?" She says in a way that makes it almost a whisper.

The sun is positioned directly behind her head, so she is eclipsed, but you are practically blinded when you look at her. You try your best not to squint when you nod your head.

"Sometimes I think about everything I missed out on when I was in prison." She bites a slice of her lip. Blood bubbles out, but it looks like it is probably an accident. "Sometimes I think about life before prison."

You place your hand on top of hers pressed firmly beside you. You move your thumb across her skin while, with her other hand, she strokes the abandoned cat.

"The space between one ear and the other gets filled with these memories."

"Like what?" You ask.

"Like Hope drawing boys' names and hearts on my jeans with markers. Alyssa dating boys when she didn't want to date at all and getting jealous when I fucked the boys after her. Kane's new tattoo when it was his first. Now he's got at least twenty. His newest tattoo when it was supposed to be my name before it wasn't. Mina's crying in the school bathroom between history and geometry. Me in the bathroom with her because I didn't go to geometry. Debby in the hallway calling into us and us pretending we couldn't hear her, even though we could." Then she stops. You see her concentrating on the things that are storming inside that space in her head and you wonder if concentrating on them is worth it. She finishes, "Hope inviting me to sleepovers. Us writing boys' names and hearts on our arms with makers. Smoking weed in Dad's truck, parked in the garage. Talking about how Lanie was a slut. Stoned on coke. Before I was a slut, stoned on coke."

You don't know any of these people, but they sound like a nice life.

You rest your head on her shoulder and think about what to say but it's like nothing's worth it.

And you can't help but wish you were a part of that storm in her mind, but she didn't know you back then. You didn't know her. There is always a time when people in our life never existed, to us, except maybe our parents and siblings who have always been there.

You hear some sort of dramatic sigh or sniffle or something that belongs in a performance.

This is the moment you think Roman's been preparing you for.

"But things aren't real," you say to her. Matter of factly.

And if she's sad, like really sad, maybe it's because she feels unacknowledged, but that's weird, because she's the one you've dropped most things for, for the past seven, ten, however many months it's been. Everything always feels like some sort of fever dream with Roman.

"You need to talk more," she says to you.

You think of Kia, who you used to talk to all the time. You think of all the things you'd say to Roman if she'd bother listening. You think of things that you have to say, but just aren't worth saying.

Roman's the type that shares anything. Has everything to teach a girl. But you've learned that you have things to teach too occasionally.

You never explained to Roman that, sometimes, a girl has to keep a secret. Like, you could've told her about the life your mother used to have. When she wore designer pumps to three dates a week with different men. When she didn't have to worry about money because she only had to pay for herself and had men who usually paid for her anyway. She got tattoos on her back that she now hides. This is a life you've only heard in stories, seen in pictures. It's not the life she lives now, because then she got pregnant and had you. Needed a real job, a house, something stable. To pick up the kid from school when she's sick. Spend extra time shopping for food or clothes or Christmas gifts when she could afford it. You could have told Roman that you're not worth what your mother had to give up. You've told secrets before. But you didn't. Tell her that.

The cat that is on her lap is now purring as Roman's hand pokes beneath it, feeling for something in the pockets of her jeans.

She pulls out a couple of sharp, needle-looking things. Curved and translucent.

"What are those?"

"Cat claws."

"That's a weird thing to carry in your pocket." You want her to know this.

She says it's time for some new art. "Scarification. A lot of cultures use it for rituals. It's like branding but easier to draw details." Her eclipsed face looks at you. "What should I draw?"

You imagine her asking what design you want, but she doesn't even ask if you want one this time. She just starts scarring herself.

She said she needs some wine for this so now you're back in the church. There is no light in this room. The colors of everything are dull, if not unseeable. Even the blood that Roman's drawing seems darker than it should be. Somewhat lost. She thinks the cat claws are clearer than a brand, but she might not even know what she's drawing now all huddled next to you in a shadow. You're not sure how the church hasn't realized it's missing so much wine.

Roman's told you before that she only showers once every two or three days maybe. But she washes her hair every time. The floor beneath you is concrete, with a red Persian rug in front of you, and even bound by this musty smell, you catch some of the rosemary that she uses.

Roman says nothing. You say nothing. The people outside of the church say nothing.

Her eyes are closed. She's not even looking at herself now as she does some sort of old-world ritual. She still doesn't ask you to participate.

And like, even though you don't want to, it's the principle of the matter.

Her breathing's slow. Her chest deep. Blood now lines her wrist and you feel so out of place, but you have to do something. Anything.

You start talking about Russian-made nesting dolls. About how your history teacher said they're often seen as a symbol of Russian femininity. About how these dolls, one uniquely painted wooden woman inside another, look like they represent a chain of mothers who are carrying on the family legacy. And still, Roman says nothing. She's in her own world.

You try again. Desperate to be there with her, you say that your history teacher is a man (what does he know?).

It's hard to see under the dimmed color, but you can faintly make out the lines of a crescent moon. Many Greek, Japanese, and Egyptian goddesses are attached to the moon. The inside of your mouth tastes like soap.

With no response from Roman, all you're thinking about now is the dead cat covered in blood you saw on this church's porch a while back. You wonder where the body went. It wasn't on the steps today.

Roman raises her arm, sucks her wrist, removes some blood. It's only seconds before the blood returns. She laughs a little, but not in the full way that people laugh when they mean it. More like in the small way that people laugh when they've lost control.

"It's perfect," she says. You smile.

Girls are like house pets. Trained young and ruthlessly into pleasing people. At first it's parents, but very quickly it becomes boys. Men. Boys and men. Sit pretty. Don't talk too loudly. Eat nicely. Please. Please. Please people. You are there for your family first, then the world. It's a mother's job to bring a girl into the family, and then to prepare her for the world. If the training works, little girls want men.

Incredibly (or maybe not), girls want men for long enough that they stop wanting themselves. Then even more incredibly (or maybe still not), everyone is okay with this.

The bleeding doesn't stop for a while. You two sit there, watching it continue until it doesn't. The bottom of Roman's shirt is all red from its use in trying to control the blood. It will never come out now.

When it finally stops, she looks at you and smiles again.

She says half-serious, half-playful, "You know, I love you."

Her wrist with the moon is red, from blood, irritated skin, and her new scratches that will soon scar. You can see that her lines are wobbly. It's a very unsteady moon.

Roman, give me a nail, you say and she raises an eyebrow at you.

"One of these?" She asks, holding up cat parts.

Yeah. One of those.

You hear her talk but you don't know what she's saying. You think she asks what you'll cut. You're going to try a lotus. You're sure it won't look good, but that's not the point.

Staring at the soft flesh on your wrist, pale, empty, you've suddenly taken a step back and are watching someone else in your body staring at your arm. You watch this girl as she digs a cat claw into your skin, Roman on the sidelines practically cheering her on. She makes one wobbly line, then another, starting some sort of lotus, and you don't even have to feel it. You just watch as it happens.

Roman told you one time that teenage girls are ruthless.

You think they are something worse. They are disillusioned. They are a bad idea.

Roman's leaning forward now, inspecting the girl's wound-in-progress like it's something to pay attention to. Her face is really close. She might get herself scratched but it looks like she doesn't even care. There's something precious, you think, about this possibility. Scarring Roman. But while you think it could be beautiful, the girl holding the claw doesn't.

You return to the moment, like you've stepped back inside yourself, and suddenly you understand the urgency of this last cut you will make. The necessity of finishing it off. Your carved skin peels open and makes you sick to your stomach. Roman waits. You hold your breath. It's just one final tear. You look at the tender meat in front of you like a butcher might and know you can do it.

You've been preparing to destroy something your whole life.

You need Wite-Out because you want to paint your nails. Your mother is using it to cover up chipped paint on the hallway baseboard.

You ask her when she will be done.

She pretends like she doesn't hear you. She keeps her hand firm and you watch her paint the same spot on the wall at least ten times.

You tell her you need it.

"You need a lot of things." She paints another streak.

"What's that supposed to mean?"

Last year, Joan called your mother a welfare queen.

You don't even talk to Joan. You're not sure why she had anything to say about your mother. When you brought this memory up to Roman, she told you girls are bitches. Right.

"No, she's not. She works," you said to Joan.

"That don't mean anything," she said casually. She looked over your shoulder at the kids surrounding you, standing in the parking lot after school. She looked them right in the eyes to give them permission to laugh. They did.

"Yeah, it means something." You glared at the kids who were laughing down at their busted tennis shoes. Only Sam Jenkins looked up at you and stared back.

Joan shook her head. You walked away. You looked back over your shoulder, called out to her, "Your mom's a pussy."

Your mother puts the cap on the Wite-out and sticks it in the pocket of her jeans. "It means exactly what it sounds like."

So you call your mother a welfare queen.

"If I'm a welfare queen," she says and pushes herself up off the ground with her palms, "It's only because of you." She leaves the hallway you stay standing in. You hear her call back to you, "Don't you forget that." The spot she was painting now noticeably rounds out from the wall. It smells like nail polish remover or something destructive and vulgar like that.

This argument with your mother reminds you of the kids at school who throw rocks off of overpasses. They pile stones in their pockets and scale the concrete ramp. The cars race below. None of the drivers, the people in trouble, even know they could be next. The kids pick the heaviest rock, drop it over the side, and run as glass windshields shatter and horns scream and stop or go or make an accordion shape as traffic piles up. The rock might never be found in this mess.

It's you. You're the kid(s). You think about this and start to lose it.

Roman's not thrilled with your choice, but the idea of setting yourself on fire sounds worse the more you think about it. You hope she'll forgive you.

She never told you to do it, but seeing Roman with hers made you want to, so you pierced your belly button. You told no one.

Until then, you had only had your ears pierced. Your mother had them done when you were just three months old. You've heard stories about her piercing her ears with a needle and some ice on her back porch when she was twelve. You wonder if that's how she pierced your ears. You have no memory of the pain, just the leftover scars.

You knew that Jerome, a guy who hung around the place Roman sometimes slept at, did piercings. You'd met him once or twice so instead of using your own needle to do this, you called him up and asked him through some fuzzy static on the other end of the phone if he could do it. All it took was a thick needle and a jeweled rod. He told you to get yourself some cleanser and you'd be fine.

You show it to Roman because you think it could be a good enough replacement for her brand idea. You think she might be proud. Instead, she says, "Cool."

You tell Roman that you need to use the bathroom and excuse yourself. All you do is wash your hands, throw some water on your face, take a deep breath, and stare at yourself in the mirror.

Things appear blurry
although you're not sure why.

You rub at your eyes with your little fingers. You look at your bare skin, so uncool, and think about the girls on your list and what they'd think about the mark, if you were to say yes. They wouldn't even notice.

You've got water splashed all over the stupid sink now and you're not sure why the hand towel is missing. You scoop the water off the counter, nearly throwing it at the wall, and then drop down into the tub where you pull your knees up to your chest and bend your forehead against them.

Roman's in your bedroom still, doing who knows what. You hear her yell at you from a distance, ask if you're okay or something. You shout that you're fine.

Roman is so fun, but demanding, in the way that girls can be. Sometimes you still have to remind yourself that Roman's actually a woman, and you're not sure why this isn't obvious.

You look down at your nails and think about how you started getting them done recently with the lunch money you were pocketing on days you skipped eating. One salon you went to had a big, red sign lit up on the arch above the door. The N's light was out so the sign said ROYAL   AILS.

You sat down in front of a woman with short, black hair, who didn't say a word to you. She grabbed your hands, put your fingers in a warm bowl of water, and started scraping away your cuticles. You watched bubbles form in the solution. She wiped off her clippers. The bell on the front door banged against it when someone came in. The woman walked to the register to ask what the person needed.

Your wet pointer finger was starting to crease like dried leather. With the cutters sitting on the table next to you, you clipped a piece of skin off at the tip and stuck it back in the bowl.

You watched the blood in the water, detached like some kind of confession. Soft and airy. It almost looked beautiful.

The woman returned, saw the blood, and gasped. You saw her shake her head as she walked away once more. You smiled.

You did it because you wanted anyone to know that someone is angry, even if there were no consequences for you doing it.

She ended up wrapping your finger in cheap paper towel and masking tape, didn't finish painting that nail, and sent you home. "Unsafe," she said. "Unsafe."

On your walk back, the blood soaked through your makeshift bandage. You passed a family on bikes. Two small children, and a man you assumed to be their father, outside a gas station. They stood over their bikes like they were trying to leave. The father had on gold-rimmed sunglasses, a baseball cap, and a chain necklace. You noticed a small razorblade hanging from the chain.

You heard the little girl standing next to him ask him for some gum. She didn't even look old enough to know how to chew it without swallowing it. The boy on her right, a little older, pulled a wad from his mouth and held it out to her in one of his palms. Dad said that wasn't good for her. There was a water gun in the wicker basket on her bike.

Past the gas station was a row of houses off the main road. In one of the garages was a parked car and a man sitting in the driver's seat, doors shut. He looked out at you like he didn't see you.

The road was under construction at that time. There was a backhoe loader parked on the side of the road. No one around to watch it.

Even though Roman says things aren't real, you couldn't help but think, "Unsafe. Unsafe."

The bathtub is smooth, cool. The color is bubblegum pink. You hear a robin outside the window. Then you notice the suction of the front door opening, the tapping of shoes, groans. Your mother.

She walks down the hall in silence except for the noise her weight makes. She enters her bedroom which is right next to the bathroom, but she has no idea where you are. Once she's shut the door, you leave the bathroom and walk the opposite way back to your room.

Roman had started drawing hearts around the stickers on your nightstand with a Sharpie while you were gone. It looks like she's now carving some into the wood with one of your metal hangers.

This reminds you of the time Roman drew a heart and a penis in thick permanent marker on a metal lamp post. You walked past it on your way to the park. You weren't sure what it meant, and were even more unsure of whether or not the public knew what it meant. Like maybe they knew something you're supposed to but don't. She stuck the marker in her back pocket, skipped a few steps to catch up with you and grabbed your hand. She nuzzled her head against your shoulder. "Men are dicks," she said. Roman never told you this, but you thought she might have started crushing on one of the guys who hung around the place she stayed. Maybe that's why she drew a heart next to a dick. It might make sense then.

You don't greet her. Say nothing about the water in the bathroom or graffiti on your bedroom furniture. Instead, you decide to tell Roman about how you ran into an old friend's dad at the video store last week and he said hi. Asked how you've been. He hasn't seen you in a while.

You had shrugged. You haven't seen his daughter Babette in a while either, and you guess that's why he hasn't seen you.

He said that's a shame. He put his hand on your back. It felt heavy, like a slaughter.

You walked away and he followed. You pretended to look at a movie you weren't interested in and he asked how you were doing. You said fine. He put his hand on your shoulder and grabbed its shape with the balls of his fingers.

You almost end the story you're telling Roman with "And then I didn't want to exist," but you stop. You consider telling her that he was too fast and too forward instead. What you end up telling her is that he winked at you.

One day, while you and Roman were walking to the Chicken Shack three blocks from your house, she said absentmindedly that, under the surface, anions are really about control.

You said, onions?

She told you no. Anions. Which are atoms that have more electrons than protons. This means they have a negative charge. This means there's too much acid in your blood. This is bad. When there's too much acid in the blood, you might experience rapid, deep breathing while the body tries to compensate for it. You might get confused. If it's severe enough, you might get shocked or die.

Yeah. Onions, you thought. Onions. If someone's allergic to onions, it can stop them from breathing (and cause blurred vision and intense itching). You know this because a kid in second grade was weirdly allergic to onions. The teacher brought in a bag of them, expecting students to make craft flowers out of the peels, but stupid Johnny started eating one of the onions like an apple, and then his throat closed up. He went to the hospital and he lived, but all the kids made fun of him after that. Including you.

It rained that morning. There were a lot of worms on the sidewalks. Roman looked at one of them. You saw it in her eyes. The desire to stomp on it. But she didn't.

Worms don't breathe through their lungs. They breathe through their skin. That's why so many are seen after a rainstorm, because the thick, wet dirt makes it hard for them to breathe, which brings them to the surface.

Roman doesn't like you ending your story on the wink. She says that's not a good ending to a story, really.

She stops scratching hearts. Asks how you responded to him. You don't think it's fair for her to ask you to tell her the truth.

When you don't respond, she looks back over her shoulder at you and closes her lips. You want to open them but know that's not right.

Then you think you must say something, but you worry that what you say might be wrong. You imagine yourself telling her the truth, that things like that make you not want to exist, but in your imagination, when you see Roman nod her head like she is listening, she actually isn't.

Instead, you don't say anything.

"Hello?? Are you there?" She waves her hand around. You shake your head. She repeats, "What did you do?"

You tell her you turned around and hugged him. He offered you a ride home and you said yes. You got in his truck. He knows what the skin of your thigh feels like. You mean tastes like. You mean both. You say you liked it.

You don't know why you lie. You're scared to say you just left.

Roman immediately scratches something different in your nightstand and now you're sure you really fucked up.

"You're lying," she says.

You tell her you're not.

You walk over to the side of the bed she's on and see that the wood where she scratched it says *guts*.

You hear your mother shout, "Who are you talking to?"

You considered following the family at the gas station back to their house just to see what kind of house they lived in. It probably wasn't far, after all, their caravan included two little kids on bikes. What you remember is slowing down just enough to turn in their direction and follow if you decided to, but then you kept on walking past when you heard the father say, "Dirty stuff like that is how you get yourself un-wifed, Jenny." He laughed because he thought he was funny. He never even yelled at the boy who was the one to give her his chewed-on gum. You no longer wanted to see their house.

Roman holds her finger against her lips. Shh.

You tell her it's okay. Don't worry about it. Your mother might pretend she gives a shit if she found out Roman was there, but wouldn't actually, although you still don't exactly want her to know anyway.

You go to grab Roman's hand like she often does to you. You miss and grab her wrist. You feel the bones in her arm.

Roman shakes her head. She doesn't even look at you. Then she turns, pokes her head out the door and moves to leave. You pull her back by the wrist. Now she looks at you. Stares. You think it might be glares. You're convinced she hates you.

You ask her where she's going.

"Gonna see if Jay's around to pick me up. Might party with the girls tonight."

You don't know who Jay is.

"You know, the guy I stay with."

This is the first time you've ever heard his name. You're a little angry that she wants to go out with 'the girls' and you're not included. You dig your right heel into the ground. All because she thinks you lied. And about some man no less.

You ask if she could do that some other time.

"And do what now?"

"Hang out with me."

You imagine her saying, "How, if you don't exist?" but there's no way she knows that's what you've been thinking. You have no idea what she actually says. You don't hear it.

She rolls her eyes. You think about telling her you've got some new eyeshadow you could play with. Or you could take her for a drive and pick up Marlboros and Patrón. What's important to her?

She shakes her head. "I'll see you later."

She leaves your room but when you follow her, poke your head out the door, you don't see her down the hall. It's like she disappeared.

Roman one time asked if you'd ever danced, and the answer was no, you hadn't. So she said come on, and her bare hand grabbed your braceleted wrist. She pulled you into your yellow kitchen in front of the dented fridge with the upper freezer and a metal bar. With Roman centered there, it was like she was a magnet meant to decorate the place. Your mother had none.

"What song do you like dancing to?"

You said, "Fuck if I know. I told you I don't dance."

Nose to nose then, she said, "You should start."

With an arm reaching behind her, she opened the fridge so just a dim light reached out and barely highlighted your ankles. Even in the still dark you noticed her belly button through her thin shirt. The ring was new. Usually a simple ball, it looked like it might be a flower that night and you wondered where she got it.

"You've got ten goddamn seconds."

You believed her.

She held her hands up as if she was conducting a song, or pulling you in to dance, so you gave her your hands. She said Goddamnit, girl. Get it together. Fucking sing like no one's listening, but you didn't know how. Not there with your mother gone. Not there with Roman holding onto you. Not there where you honestly couldn't see anything. Where the neighbor's dog was out back barking because they never let it in. Never. Not where all you could think about was how Roman was a goddamn magnet in a kitchen the size of a small bathroom and, suddenly, this woman expected you to be a singer and dancer all at once.

You think about her stained fingers reaching out for your hand at the gas station, about the nights she drank wine from a bottle in the back of the cathedral. You think about her hair. You think about her freckles, the mud stains on her jeans. About the way she fit into your collarbones when she wanted to. You think about her punching the guy who fucked her sister. You think about her crying over the bruises on her knuckles. You think about the days you've missed school, about the days she showed up unannounced. Your mother will never meet her. Not now, not ever. You think about the slow and languid way she moved. About how now you're not sure who to tell that, just like that, Roman's gone.

You realize you'll miss hearing, "So tell me a secret."

You start spinning the bar in your belly button despite the pain that surges through your body.

You turn and look around the room. For the first time since returning from the bathroom, you realize that your bedroom is spotless. Like no one ever existed in it. The brand-new sheets tucked. Pillows on top. Clothes picked up off the floor. Makeup brushes placed in drawers. Even your alarm is more centered than usual.

Your mother calls, yells in the way you would have expected Roman to, but she says, "I'm getting pizza for dinner." She says nothing when you don't respond.

You sit on the edge of your bed. Keep playing with the bar in your belly button. You never told Roman this, because it looked good on her, but you've always hated jewelry. You've just always understood that you must wear it as a woman.

The front door slams as your mother leaves once more.

You heard a news story last week about a girl who ran away. You missed the girl's name. The news anchor hoped the girl was watching (although you know that if you ran away from home, the last thing you'd be doing is watching the news). Assuming she was, he spoke to her, and begged her to return. Then her mother, crying muddy tears, mascara melted down her cheeks, spoke to the daughter. She said she missed her. She said through wet words televised to the whole world, please come home.

You think about how if you were ever inconvenienced with a daughter, one who ran away, you'd let her.

You wouldn't have known that the woman on the news ever existed if it wasn't for her fucked up daughter. Women only get noticed when they're pregnant/of child/have a kid. No one cares for them until then. Then people care enough.

For most people, caring is just some kind of excuse to tell women what to do.

While you wait in the kitchen for your mother to return, you notice the calendar nailed to the wall. You realize your birthday was two days ago. Everyone missed it. Even you.

You take a pen from the junk drawer and cross off the days from last week, including your birthday.

Roman told you once that reality is never the same. All those things that are permanent can't be real because they're all just made up.

You start crossing off all the calendar days. Even the ones that haven't happened yet. Line, scribble, dash. The calendar starts to become so black it's unreal. You wonder if days feel like this to the runaway girl. You wonder if nylons you've seen left on the main mile road belong to anyone. You wonder if forcing someone to exist, just to die, is important.

You hear your mother's car pull up in the driveway. Squeaking breaks. Tires against concrete. This tells you that you're no longer alone.

Roman told you once she was never named Roman. She was named something else. She named herself. You think of the things that girls you never knew signed in your school yearbook each year: NEVER CHANGE. In pencil. In pink gel pen with hearts. In permanent marker. It's always more than one. Always girls. You pull your two-sizes-too-big-because-one-day-it-will-shrink gym shirt up. Can't remember the last time you went to gym class. With one hand, you dig your fingers into the soft meat of your belly, the loud nightmare of your body. You hold onto your belly button ring with two fingers and spin it in circles. It stings. You plan to tell your mother that you want to be called something different. Something tempting. This will probably change.

The front door opens. Keys drop to the floor. Door doesn't shut. Your mother enters the kitchen with a sweaty fifth of vodka in her hand. Exhaling. She says pizza is in the car or something. The way she treads the house in her dollar-store flip flops sounds like a couple of girls playing patty cake and naming off the ones they hate. She heads to her room.

You wish you could tell Roman you understand now. What you have doesn't matter.

What you're given matters even less.

You are reminded of the time Roman asked you when your birthday was. She said that if you took her to the store that day, she'd get supplies to make you a picnic. You two could sit out at a park during sunset. You didn't like the idea of eating in front of kids playing and parents watching nearby, and didn't want people to think you two were lovers or something. She added, "Fuck the kids playing on the playground. Life goes on, even when everyone's around you."

When you laughed, Roman said, "I promise." She even gave you her pinky.

You told her it would be nice.

You two never did go to the store.

You care about Roman but, on second thought, have to admit that it probably doesn't make much sense to miss her.

"I'm not going back to my place," you say to Roman. Something makes you reach across Roman to grab Evan's hand. You tell her that you're talking to Evan right now. You nod at him and see him smile a little from your peripherals.

"But it's getting late," Roman whines. She pouts. She rubs her hand up your bare thigh since your skirt keeps moving higher and higher up your leg.

You say, I know.

"Fine. I'll go find someone else." She rolls off you and the couch and clumsily wanders back up the stairs. When she opens the door at the top, you hear a whole other world's noise, music, shouting, singing, or something, flood the much quieter basement. Then she shuts the door. Then it's gone.

Your necklace is twisted again.

"She seems special," Evan says once she's left. You can't tell if he's joking or not. She is.

"Yeah."

He starts to rub his own hand down your thigh, but it feels different than Roman. He doesn't rub it back up.

"You're special too. In a different way," he adds.

You say thanks. You scratch a spot on your arm. You don't know what else to say.

"You're probably too young for me, but I'd love to go on a date. Would you like that? To go on a date tomorrow night?"

Things start to feel fuzzier than they already do. You fix your necklace again and take a hard look at Evan. Evan, who is probably in his mid-twenties and handsome and has dark hair that swoops a little. He's got those long guy-dimples that start at the cheeks and curve under the lips. His eyes are blue.

You ask, "What do you have in mind?" You've never been on a date before.

Roman has told you her birthday is New Year's Eve. She said, "If you don't mind sharing your birthday, being born on New Year's Eve is fantastic. There will always be a party, which is more than what some people have, for celebrating their birth." You're not sure if you believe her. You had already given her a birthday gift in August when she told you then that her birthday was coming up. Sometimes you think every day is Roman's birthday in her mind.

You always thought a man would fix your sadness.

"Let's do dessert. Do you like ice cream?"

It's okay, but you prefer cake. In the back of your head you hear Roman saying that ice cream's a fun sex toy. Cake seems like it would make a terrible sex toy.

You decide that Evan will work.

"All right. That sounds good."

You're grateful that you don't sound overly eager. That would be very uncool.

You think back to the time that Roman told you to become god, a god, your own god – she said something about god, and god doesn't pass up opportunities, right?

Evan smiles at you and the dimples poked into his face grow. He's got really nice lips. Kissable.

And a ring on his finger. You start to breathe shallow. Your throat. Your eyes. You tell Evan it's late and you should go home.

He yawns. "Yeah, I should head out too. Don't want to sleep through our date." He kind of winks. You kind of smile.

"Can I get your number?"

The last time a boy asked for your number, it was a joke, but Evan's not a boy. This must be different.

You and Roman were leaving a 7/11, Slurpees in hands (yours was blue raspberry and hers was Sour Patch pineapple mixed with cherry). Like a movie, you heard music playing. Unsure of the song, but it felt upbeat. And romantic. Out of practically nowhere, a young couple fluttered by you, dancing. It looked like swing dancing, from what you've seen in the movies. They were in wedding outfits: him, black slacks, a white button-up, and a suit coat. Her, a short, flirty, white dress with lace lining its short sleeves. Her hair was pinned up in curls. Roman took a sip of her vile drink, and as the couple danced to some music playing from a boombox in the 7/11 parking lot, they looked happy. You took a sip of your drink. Your tongue was blue.

"I went to Urgent Care to get a checkup, thought I had bronchitis, and they said something's wrong. So I said, all right. Let's get it fixed."

And that's how Evan ended up finding out his heart function was at ten percent at the age of twenty. He needed a heart transplant.

He tells you this as you two sit next to each other at the ice cream shop where he's eating a vanilla cone and you're drinking a strawberry milkshake. You're thinking of what Roman said, and of Evan's thick lips, and of him licking the pink off your bare skin, lying in bed. Not your bed. Maybe his bed. But then you think of his wife.

"How did your heart get so bad?" You lift your straw to your lips and let it press against the bottom one. You look at Evan expectantly.

"A virus. They don't know what kind."

Oh.

Evan doesn't notice your lips. You look at his chest and think about the scar he must have over his heart. Someone else's heart.

There was a time a few months ago when you and Roman got ice cream. She got a raspberry sundae with extra whipped cream, a cherry, and chocolate drizzled on top. You got a vanilla milkshake. You bought both.

A middle-aged man with a chocolate cone walked past the table you two were sitting at. Roman told you to try a bite of her sundae, but just a bite, no more, she wanted most of it, but the raspberries were *de*-lectable. You shook her off, told her your milkshake was fine. It was also de*lect*able (you put emphasis on the word differently) and she scooped her ice cream, missing the raspberries, trying to spoon-feed it to you.

The man stopped. Looked right at you and said, "I recognize those perrty lips, but my memory is a bit rusty with old age. Did we ever make out back in the day at Jimmy MacDonald's house?"

Back in the day, you were a child. A real child.

Details get lost.

Before you said anything, Roman laughed at the man.

The building's floor was left over from a few decades ago. Green and gray tiles. The tables were wooden and wobbly. The man had a hunting coat on even though it was not that cold outside. Tan work boots. Callused hands. His lips were thin and mostly covered by a mustache that hadn't been styled in a long while. None that you'd ever want to kiss.

"Get out of here, dude," Roman threatened. She whispered to you that she might try and hit him with some of her sundae.

He smirked. Some ice cream in his mustache. He opened his mouth to say something, but you went first. "The answer's no. I'm way too young for you."

"And hot," Roman added.

First you looked at her. Your cheeks turned apple-red. Then you looked away, trying to hide the burn.

The man started shouting fucker and hoe at you as an employee walked out to the lobby. Roman and you laughed and scrambled out the door as she carried her Styrofoam bowl, trying not to spill what was in it.

"What about you? Any health scares?"

"Nothing like that." You've been lucky with your health, thankfully.

"Good thing. It sucks." He chuckles lightly. He's almost done with his cone. Luckily Evan has no beard or mustache so there's nothing left behind.

You shrug and take another sip of your milkshake, still imagining what it might taste like against your skin. You are not going to tell Evan this though. His eyelashes are long.

"There's this study I heard of," he starts to tell you, "Where there's like, thirty-something questions that if you ask each other, will make you fall in love."

You're down to the last bit of shake in your cup. You suck until the cup inhales itself, making an obnoxious noise.

With a mouthful of ice cream, you go, "Hmm." You swallow. Add, "Sounds interesting. Like voodoo magic or something."

"I've never tried it with anyone, but could be cool."

"Could have interesting results," you add. Like an experiment.

If he is suggesting that you two play this question game like you think he is, you're not sure why. You wonder if he is trying to fall in love with you.

Then again, maybe the study, this question game, is wrong. Love always is.

You were in front of your mirror, getting ready to go out one Saturday night. Roman was behind you, leaning over your shoulder, making your reflection look like your body had a second head. You'd already done your makeup. You were trying to figure out what to do with your hair.

You'd seen a Gucci ad recently. The woman was wearing bright pink tights, white strappy heels, a fitted, white, knee-length skirt and a purple, long-sleeve crop top. You felt like it was a little daring for you, so you did your best to recreate it at the thrift shop, but without the tights.

In your ear, like she was the angel on your shoulder, Roman said, "What are you going for tonight?"

The two of you were meeting up with some of her friends from her man-boy's house. They were all older, cocaine users, and dressed nicer than you. You wanted to impress them at least.

There was also this guy Robert who'd be there. Roman talked about him all the time. He was in the military. Is out of the military. Hangs around the women at that house but doesn't make a pass on any of them. His favorite color is green, like, a Kelly green. He drinks Sprite constantly. He sounds kind of charming. You wouldn't mind meeting him.

Roman's still next to your ear like an angel. You feel her breath on your skin, and she's looking at you straight in the eyes via the mirror you're both standing in front of. Your hands above your head, holding your hair up like you might put it in a ponytail. Roman whispers, "I want your life to be more than a sex movie. Make it something bigger. Better."

You never got to meet Robert.

"It could be fun to try it. I mean, let's just see if this study is based on science."

It could be interesting. "For science," you say.

He grins. "I've got the questions back at the house."

"Would you want to be famous?"

You two are sitting on his bed, you with crossed legs, him with his legs straight out. You're supposed to look right at each other as you answer these questions. For science.

You genuinely think about your answer, and aren't sure which one is right. Yes or no. You tell Evan, "Maybe. I don't know. Being famous seems like a lot of work, emotionally draining even, but it also seems like it'd be nice to be acknowledged. For people to know you exist. To care about you, I guess."

Evan nods his head in an understanding way. You ask him back if he'd like to be famous. He says no, but if he had to, he'd want it to be for some cool skateboarding tricks - that he'd have to learn first. The two of you laugh at this. His skin is somehow perfect and it makes you self-conscious of the two pimples on your chin that were too hard to cover up.

The questions are divided up into three sections, getting increasingly personal. In section two, he asks you, "What is most important to you in a friendship?" And immediately you think of Roman, then feel bad about Kia, and then have to figure out your answer.

"Someone who genuinely cares about me," you say simply. You don't know if this exists.

You're not sure what Evan's response is. You're looking around his bedroom.

Over a half-hour later, in section three, Evan says, "What do you like about me? It says to be honest and tell me something you probably wouldn't say to someone you've just met," but you're busy noticing for the first time the pictures of the two of them sitting on the dresser. Evan's wife is pretty, but has indistinct features. You're not sure you could recognize her. If someone else looked like her, you're not sure you'd know the difference. You wonder how she might respond to this question if Evan was asking her it instead.

Evan waves his hand in front of your face like you're absent. He says, "I know it's hard to come up with only one thing. Please, if you need to list more, don't stop yourself." He smiles.

You bow your head and giggle softly.

"I like how calm you make me feel," you say as he uses his pointer finger to gently lift your chin up so you're looking him in the eyes as you finish your sentence.

"That's nice," he says.

You ask him the question back. Evan lowers his hand, putting both of them behind him, so he's leaning back on them casually.

"I like," he starts dramatically – pauses for some sort of effect – then adds, "That you're authentic."

You aren't sure how. He doesn't know you enough to know if you're authentic. Everything you say could be a lie. Sometimes it is. He must get authenticity and wariness confused.

You were grocery shopping by yourself last week and Alyssa walked past you. Alyssa was a friend you haven't spoken to since middle school. You heard last year that she had a kid, although no one even knows who the father is. She's tiny, so it was hard to picture her with a pregnant body, but one day in the hallway you saw her, pregnant as shit.

There in the grocery store, she had a shopping cart full of vegetables, diapers, and formula. Was wearing a long dress made of what looked like quilt fabric and that closed by buttons down the center.

She's the same person you remember, except now she looks like a mom. Like she's playing house and that role makes sense.

Evan raises his hands to both sides of your jaw and pulls you two nose-to-nose. The experiment isn't finished. "Can I kiss you?" He asks. You can feel the pressure of his fingers against your skin, holding up your cheeks.

You know it is wrong to not answer him, especially after wanting this so badly, but when you don't respond, he smiles that charming smile and you close your eyes like this for the first time (turn to page 152). You're out of breath.

You are tense as he rolls his hand up your spine – under your shirt of course. His face is buried in your shoulder and you look past him at the pictures you just noticed hanging on the wall next to the closet door. Why didn't you see those earlier?

In these pictures particularly, his wife was, is, gorgeous. Way prettier than you. Why is he even interested in you? It is because you're young. That has to be it. Maybe he'll do things to you that he can get away with because you won't tell him no. Maybe his wife says no.

She is in a little black dress. She has a tiny waist, hourglass, like you aren't. Her hair has volume, her cheeks glow, and her knees aren't knobby like yours. She doesn't need tights like you to cover up a scar on your calf from a childhood fight with a kid down the block.

Evan pulls his hand away from you and looks at your vacant face.

"Is everything okay?" He asks.

You start to shrug, then stop. "Yes, I'm fine."

He has no smile. "I don't want this if you don't enjoy it," he says.

"I do."

He is not convinced.

Evan leans back a little, looking disappointed, and starts to button up his shirt when you stop him. You grab his hand, say, "I mean it. I do. I want this."

"Then what's the problem? You feel a million miles away."

You decide not to tell him that you are imagining his wife naked, with a tight body, like women in advertisements, thin. Although he might be into the idea of you imagining his naked wife. Instead you tell him "I'm sorry."

Evan looks over his shoulder. Must see the pictures. "Is it Lena?" he asks. Lena is his wife.

"No," you say defensively. You wish he'd just stop asking questions and fuck you. Is this what it feels like to be in a relationship?

Your eyes are wide and soft like a doe's but you lean into his chest and notice his smell. He smells like fresh linen and man.

"I do really love the way you are authentic."

Your mother asked you where you'd been the last few months because you never seemed to be home anymore one morning before school. You answered with, "Neither are you." She was packing her lunch in a blue sack with Velcro to close it.

"I don't need that attitude."

You rolled your eyes and grabbed a honey and nut granola bar from the cupboard above her lunch.

"What are your plans for today?" She asked.

You took a bite of your bar and shrugged your shoulders. Act cool. Like you don't know your plans yet, but they could get busy. Like you're on call for plans. But really, you knew that Roman wanted to be driven up to the movie theater where she suggested you two pay for one movie then spend the rest of the night rotating through others. Like Russian roulette but with entertainment.

"I'll be at work late tonight. TV dinners are in the freezer. Please come home – have a night in. I expect to see you when I get back. Do your homework."

Sure.

You and Evan didn't fuck that night. Even after you tried to open his lips with your tongue, slide between his teeth, he pushed you away and repeated, "I mean it. I don't want this if you don't enjoy it." You could've sworn you seemed like you were enjoying it.

Instead, he buttoned his shirt and invited you to play a card game with him. Go Fish. You told him you had other things to do. You weren't sure when his wife was coming home anyway and you sure didn't want to be there when that happened.

It was easier to pretend she didn't exist.

In another world, you'd have asked him to take down her photos.

You worked as a line server at a restaurant for seven months before you met Roman. You stopped working there a month after. Because it was tough to keep a job or because it seemed meaningless to have one. You're not sure. But Roman encouraged the quit, said you could hang out together that much more and reminded you that customers were the devil anyway. Are you asking for a one-way ticket to Hell?

You weren't.

Two men came into the restaurant one night you still worked there. One of them walked up to the line, ordered his food, got down to the register where you were, and he looked at the fake tattoo star you had stuck under your eyes and said, "Is that real?"

You and Kia used to put fake tattoos on each other all the time, wetting the other's skin with a paper towel and adhering hearts and swallows to different parts of your bodies. Usually your back, upper arm, or thigh. This was the first time you did it to yourself and put it somewhere visible.

You told the guy, no. They weren't real.

The dude asked, "It's fake? Really?"

And all you had to say was, Yup.

You'd cashed the man out already. Handed him his bag of food, but he still stood there talking to you.

"Where'd you get it from?

Meijer.

"Yeah? Really? What? The twenty-five-cent machine?"

No.

Some kind of silence while he waited for more.

You gave it to him like you're supposed to. "I bought a kit of four hundred for ten bucks."

"Oh. Your school lets you wear that?"

You wished a short line would begin to form behind him, to push him along, but you were past the dinner rush. It was just him and his friend in the distance waiting for him in the restaurant.

"Well, I'm not in school this week, we're on break, but yeah."

Incredulously, "It's Spring break already?

You corrected him: "Winter."

"Oh. You go to that school down the street?"

"Yeah." He didn't need to know that. But you added, "We've got kids who have real tattoos."

You're just a simple girl. This is fake anyway, mister.

"But not on their face." He was stuck.

"Yeah, no, I guess not. I don't know."

The man finally took his foil-wrapped burrito and walked away. You couldn't tell what he was wearing beneath his winter coat, but his pants were khaki and fitted. Next to the drink machine, he, probably in his late twenties or early thirties, greeted another man, probably in his late thirties or mid-forties. The new guy was wearing a plaid, unbuttoned shirt, a split-end ponytail, and missing two front upper teeth. He looked like the type of person to have plastic lawn chairs on his front lawn and a boat out back if he could afford it. He hadn't ordered anything. Said to the first guy, "She's cute! Why didn't you get her number?"

"Dude, she's in high school."

You're not sure high school mattered. It was probably the tattoos that kept him from asking you out. He didn't seem to understand they were fake.

Evan did reach back out to you after that first night, despite you acting like such a baby. You made sure not to think too hard (or at all) the next time.

One day after school Evan called to say he'd like to see you. You had to buy a ticket to the Christmas talent show first since rumor had it some kids were supposed to play a prank on the principal there but told him you'd come over after. He answered his door with his ring on like usual and offered you a beer before saying he'd like to move to the bedroom.

Lying in the folds of his sheets you were all skin. Completely naked except your socks he did not take off and they stuck to you. The meat of his palms pushed against your body. He felt potent. He said he missed you, had been waiting for you, or something. He pressed his crescent-parted lips against your neck and his teeth left a mark. His skin left a track of sweat across you. You felt warm. He dragged his thumb down your hips and started to peel you as if you were a blood orange. Fresh. You had watched porn once and figured the small breathless noises you gasped made a sound like you enjoyed it so he never stopped you, or asked if you enjoyed it, again. You kept your mouth open and your eyes closed and it felt not like people say it does but just like you imagined it might.

You now alternate the days you spend with Roman with the days you fuck Evan. You don't tell her that though. You think about it but decide she doesn't need to know. She does things she doesn't tell you about after all. You still don't know what she does at that pimp's house with all the other women. You can't decide if it's just nights of cocaine, or secrets in ears, or naked sex scenes, or all of the above. Or none. She's never said. This leaves a lot of room to make things up.

So you spend fewer nights with her. But when you do spend nights with her, it's usually lying in your bed together, telling stories.

"Imagine a girl signed up for a psychological experiment. She's told to steal a wallet from a coworker's purse and not get caught. She does it – goes to the closet with the purse, heart racing, freaking out because she's never stolen something before, then does it. Steals the wallet from the coworker, but it was on a desk. Not in the purse. She returns to the study and finds out she stole the wrong one."

You two laugh at the story. At how the girl stole the wrong thing. Like what you steal matters when you're stealing.

Then you say, "Whole people scare me. Like, you're a whole person. You ever look at pictures of your parents as kids? Or like, from before they had you? Yeah. A whole person. Then it's like, she's not just your mom anymore." You'd never seen real childhood pictures of your mother. She never showed you them.

She says, "That's not a story."

"You're lying," you say. Seriously though.

You spend nights with Evan. These are nights that Lena works. She's a nurse at a hospital far away and works twelve-hour evening shifts which keep her busy. That may be why she gives Evan permission to sleep with other people.

He always takes you on dates before taking off your shirt to gaze at your breasts. He says yours are bigger than Lena's but you know that's not true from the pictures. You wonder what else he lies to you about.

One day he took you to the casino. Got you in by telling them you two were going to the restaurant in the back, which you were. You just ended up at a few slot machines on the way there.

When going home, you stopped so he could get cigarettes. You didn't know he smoked. He said only casually. Sometimes. Not frequently. But he was out and did need to stock up.

Something about this addiction made him sexier.

Days like that, you end up back at his place after. You see Lena's little love notes left on the counters and pictures with her on the walls, and you still close your eyes tight – you never thought you'd be someone to close your eyes when having sex – and you kiss him like someone you've known before.

You've still not met Lena. You also never stopped to think about how her dress in the photo is made to make women sexy. You don't know the shape of her body underneath it.

It's been over four months since that party you met Evan at, that party Roman invited you to. Where he asked, "You gonna give that back?" and where you said, "I wasn't planning on it."

Now he's got you in the shower. He's had sex with you on the bed, the kitchen counter, and the living room floor. It started sweet, then got less sweet. He says the new spots, new techniques, are like upgrades. The shower is new. He stepped in first. Stands there naked but holds his hand out and invites you in like you have a choice. You know you don't. He tells you it's better wet, then he winks. When you join him he almost immediately starts rubbing soap down your body. Lathers you. He tries to enter you but you're worried that you'll slip and fall so you can't keep your leg high enough. He says it's okay but looks disappointed. He asks if you can give him head. He thinks sitting in the shower on your knees, water streaming down your face, filling your mouth, is better.

His hair is longer than when you met him. You tell him you like his longer hair. No, he tells you. It's too long. You tell him you like his too-long hair. He's getting it cut soon, he says. It's annoying.

You are overcome with exhaustion, next to him in his bed. You don't mean to spend the night and wake up late. When you do wake up, he asks if you'd like a ride to school (turn to page 163) but you could also just say no (turn to page 186).

There's a community pool near Evan's house. It's empty right now and cannot be used even though no one knows why. You two watched some kids scale the sides on skateboards.

He told you about the time a friend took him to the First Baptist Church parking lot to sell someone a gun. The friend pulled a black tackle-looking box from his trunk. You're sure it wasn't a tackle box, and you don't even have to know anything about fishing to know that.

Evan said he didn't do anything except watch the exchange. He knows nothing about shooting or selling a gun.

You thought about how you could probably cannibalize all your memories and he would just watch that too.

You noticed cop cars sitting outside a house down the block. This made you two leave the pool, even if the boys you were watching were still skating down the vacant slopes, despite looming danger.

You didn't tell them. They'd figure it out on their own.

You leave Evan's house and don't say bye.

Evan said he'd call you, but you don't want it. You've learned it's for the best. When people just forget us and we just forget them. You know this truth.

It turns out it was never a real date.

You regret agreeing to the ride.

Evan says, "Lena's shifts are changing at work. A day shift opened up so she'll be switching to that." He drives like a soccer dad.

"Okay," you say. You pretend your fingers are in your ears. You pretend Lena doesn't exist.

"That means my schedule won't be the same."

He means he'll see her at night now. You think an open relationship means that he can date other people, regardless of his wife's schedule, but what do you know.

You think about how you were just a toy.

You expect Evan to state what he's getting at clearly, but he doesn't. There's a block of silence between you for most of Twenty Mile before he starts talking about entertainment.

"It's great when backup singers are equally as good as leads." He says this because he watched some singer perform on some late-night show yesterday, and he's convinced that the row of three singers in back sounded perfect. How is it even possible for three people to sound perfect at once?

You can't help but think backup singers are never as good as leads, or they'd be on their own from the start.

Evan laughs.

"You see that bumper sticker?" He points to the car driving in front of you.

The sticker has a clear background that just shows a white, Times New Roman font saying "If you're gonna ride my ASS at least pull my hair" on the car's back window. There's a silhouette of a curvy woman, also completely white, standing next to the phrase. She's holding her hair and sticking out her ASS.

"Yeah."

He chuckles again, but lighter than his previous laugh. "I like it," he says.

Of course he does.

Evan has wanted to pull your hair, but that's one thing you have said no to.

"I'm sorry," you told him when he asked if he could. It would hurt and you'd rather not hurt for any reason, whether you're having sex or doing anything else.

"Nah, it's all good," he said. Really.

He has respected your choice. He swears he doesn't want anything if you won't enjoy it again, but you're sure he's disappointed. Now you're like Lena, probably, saying no.

This car is going kind of slow, like the woman wants you to really ride her ass, so Evan goes to pass her. You're in the lane next to her now, about to get ahead of the car, and you look at the driver. He's a middle-aged man with aviators and a windbreaker.

You have caught rides to school with Evan sometimes before too. Sometimes you drive yourself. Sometimes you don't go at all. You sleep in and spend the last of your money that you have saved from your job on things to drink, gas for your car, and Roman.

After nights with Roman, you sometimes stay awake for twenty-four hours, mostly biting the insides of your mouth. You lose sleep. Roman has never asked you to do cocaine, you haven't done it yet, but you feel like you're picking up the habits of a coke addict through her anyway.

The nights you stay up leave you seeing stars. At least you think they're stars. Stars, or saucers thrown across the sky. Sometimes you think they rip the sky open, but other nights you're sure it's just an altostratus cloud.

You'll hear songs on a turned-off radio. Sometimes you are across from Roman who just stares at the ceiling. You ask her if she hears the radio too and she laughs. Then you realize that it's just you singing the same songs you sang to Roman on a night you danced around your kitchen. You'd never sang before that night. She laughs some more.

On almost every Wednesday evening now you spend time with Roman's crew. You had hoped there'd be more guys there, but you found yourself enjoying the majority girl-to-boy ratio instead.

You've started wearing white tank tops or t-shirts and boyfriend jeans (actual jeans from Evan's closet – you don't think he knows you took them and you're kind of surprised they mostly fit if you roll them up). Your hair is unruly so you keep it in a messy ponytail which makes it look cooler.

Boys at school still won't talk to you, but they look now. You think the looks are a good kind. The girls at school still ignore you, except for Jessica who's new to your geometry class. She doesn't know that the others don't like you.

She's the only one you've told about Evan. She thinks you're so cool for dating an older man.

"How did you meet him?" She begs to know while she eats a ham and cheese sandwich at lunch. You shrug and pop your gum pretty loud.

"A party." You dig your tongue into the inside of your cheek, look to the left with your eyes. Like there's no way you could admit this to her, this is a top secret you're revealing, even though you've really been dying for someone to know about Evan.

"What happened?"

Your mind spins through stories you could tell her, but you just tell her the truth. You took a cup of beer during his beer pong game.

She squeals kind of. Taps your arm. Opens her eyes wide. She thinks you're cooler than you are.

Perfect.

You don't tell her that you took the cup because you didn't know where the alcohol was.

You are not too far from school now, but Evan took his sweet time getting there this morning. The dashboard clock says you are already late. You might as well not even bother. You could just go home and drink some of the orange extract you've got hidden in your underwear drawer. Roman told you that $3.50 bottles of orange extract at the grocery store have 84% alcohol in them and can get you sloppy drunk. You stocked up.

Evan puts his hand on your lap. "Ready to start your day?"

This feels like an afterschool special.

Also, the answer depends on how you're starting it.

Jessica asks for your advice on everything. She calls you after school and wants to talk about first hour, and then wants your guidance on clothes, and then needs your opinion on boys. Sometimes you don't answer the phone and tell her you were busy with Evan, even if you weren't. You don't tell Roman about her. You can't tell if Roman would think you're cooler because Jessica practically drools all over you, or if she'd think you're a loser because another high school girl wishes she had your sex life with a guy who is probably using you.

It's still early morning and dawn hasn't quite painted colors in the sky yet. The world is denim blue, street lamps, and a soft light starting to make things visible. The school feels empty in the parking lot, even though you know there's too many people inside.

His hand is still on your lap.

"Okay. Thanks. Have a good day," you say as you open the door.

"Wait."

Your breath balloons inside your throat. The streetlamp nearest Evan's car starts to flicker. There are swarms of bugs circling the light.

"I want-"

"I'm already late, Evan. I'll see you later!" You push the door quickly and find yourself under a streetlamp spotlight as you leap out. You're wearing the same clothes you wore last night but since it's Monday, no one at school will know.

You power walk toward the building where you see security sitting at their table near the front door. You hear Evan's steps behind you. His car still parked in the circle drive. It's not shut off. Headlights paint the concrete ahead.

Classroom windows are all open about fifty feet from you on your left. You hear classes in session. Evan has jogged fast enough to catch up with you. He grabs your shoulder to turn you around and you almost shout at him but security has your other shoulder now and pulls you away.

Officer Julie, in her blue-collared-button-up and black belt on her thick work pants looks like a bear in front of Evan. She growls like one too.

"Who are you?" Gruff.

You think she wants to tell him he's arrested but she doesn't have that authority. You're not sure what high school security guards actually do. Can do.

"Look, I'm-"

You finish for him, "He's just leaving. He wanted to ask if I had my lunch, but I don't. I forgot it."

"Right." Evan lowers his chin.

You do not have a lunch. Didn't even think about it this morning when you were looking for your underwear and a sock.

"I'm going to need some ID," Julie persists.

"Can I have some lunch money?" You ask Evan.

His lips are a straight line. You watch him dip his hand in the pocket of the jeans you returned to his place just yesterday. He must not have realized they had been missing. You watch the shape of his hand inside the denim run over his thigh as he feels for coins and you think about the way he fucked you last week. How he moaned deep in his throat. How you screamed because he must like it.

The streetlamp shuts off.

Jessica told you about her first boyfriend. She was thirteen. Her first kiss was in his basement during Spin the Bottle. She didn't want to do it. But she did it. She did it in the middle of a circle of other kids just there to dare and to watch.

She said the boy had a tattoo and a birthmark. You asked how old he was and she said fourteen. You said you'd never seen a fourteen-year-old with a birthmark.

The tattoo was small. His older brother did it in some back-alley, prison kind of way. It's supposed to be a four-leaf clover, but Jessica said it looked kind of like the birthmark. That little black blob on his neck made Jessica want to get her own tattoo though. But she's sixteen like you and still doesn't have one.

They dated for five months. She didn't find out until after they broke up that he'd went on wild drives with his friends to meet up with other girls that he'd say, way later, were just friends, but how was she supposed to know. The night of Fourth of July, they sat on a picnic blanket underneath the city fireworks. The boy wore skinny jeans and a long-sleeved shirt and a hoodie and rubber bracelets and had just gotten his lip pierced and couldn't kiss her. Jessica asked him if he even liked kissing her, and she asked that because she knew what he was thinking, you guess. He said yeah. Sure, he liked kissing her. He reminded her that he had promised he'd do anything for her in the way that thirteen, sorry, fourteen-year-old boys do. Sorry eighteen-year-old boys. Sorry twenty-something. Boys. Guys. You don't know anymore.

She said she might have believed him but she wouldn't be allowed to kiss him for a while anyway on account of the hole in his lip, so she broke up with him even though she cried about it for a few weeks.

You wish you had a boyfriend story like that.

She said she kept all the pictures though. The boy has got a kid now and she thinks he's been to jail. Or maybe just barely avoided jail. It was a rumor she heard, but she might have believed it. Sometimes when she misses the absence of someone who could be there, she looks at the pictures of a boy who hadn't yet fallen apart. Not completely. Doing this always hurts her, but she does it anyway.

You realize you don't have any pictures you've taken with Evan. None to look back at when you miss him. None to even burn.

You don't know Jessica's ex-boyfriend, but you wonder what he's up to now, like if he's killed anyone, or if he wants to kill anyone.

You've wondered what the women of serial killers think when they find out that's who they're married to. They had to have known, right? How could they not have known the person they married?

Evan calls you over and over after school. You don't answer it until your mother gets home and answers it for you. You hear her in the front room saying, "Yeah, she's in her bedroom. I'll get her for you."

You sit on your closet floor. Shut the door. Hope she won't find you in there. In case she does, you will pretend you're looking for a missing shoe.

"Honey," your mother says when she opens the door.

You can hear her glance around the room when she can't obviously find you.

Then you sneeze. Damn it. Closet door opens.

"What are you doing in here?"

"Looking for a shoe."

"Do you need a flashlight or something?"

"No, I'm fine."

You run your hand along where the interior wall meets the floor like you're searching.

"You sure?"

"Yes."

Your mother starts to bend, as if she plans to search with you, but then hands you the phone instead. "Someone's on the phone for you. Here, take it."

"Can you tell them I'm busy?"

The two of you hear Evan yelling through the receiver, "*I can hear you!*"

Your mother looks at you like you both know the answer. She hands you the phone.

You stay in the dark closet. Answer, "Hi."

"Hey. I just wanted to talk to you. What happened earlier?"

You shrug. Evan can't see it, so he doesn't know.

"Hello?" He asks.

"Yeah, I'm here."

"Seriously. What happened earlier?"

You say, "I was late to class."

Evan laughs. "When have you ever been concerned about that?"

You don't answer but you think about how there was one time when you would have been concerned about that.

"I wanted to talk to you," he says.

And that's exactly what you didn't want. Don't want. You consider hanging up the phone and ignoring him the rest of the night. A cotton dress hanging above you falls into your face.

"Okay, but I'm sort of busy right now. Can we do this a different time?"

You hope that by putting this off you can avoid the inevitable. Like the decomposing meat Roman told you about. If you throw it out, you don't have to acknowledge it. It doesn't exist. But you also know that by putting this off, you would no longer see him until you have the conversation that he wants. Your relationship would be only in your imagination.

"No, I think we should do this now."

Fine.

"Can you meet up?" Evan asks.

You don't think you said anything out loud, but maybe you did. He starts talking like you said yes.

The last thing you want to do is this right now. Whatever conversation he wants.

You'd rather fuck him on his queen size bed, with the sheets on the floor, your bare feet tangled against his. You'd even let him pull your hair. You almost feel desperate for him to pull your hair.

"Do you want to pull my hair?" You ask him.

"What? Oh, no. That's not what this is about. We need to talk."

For a moment you were hoping violence was all he was looking for. You mean sex. You mean something sexy. You don't know anymore. What is anybody looking for?

"Where?" You ask. Although, in fact, you don't actually care where.

"Can you come over?"

You answer his question with a question. "Is Lena there?"

Evan told you on one of your first dates about how, when he was in high school, his mother had gotten their house foreclosed. She'd stopped paying the mortgage for months, years, he's not sure, and when they threatened her, she told him she was going to write "Fuck you" in blood-red paint on the wall before they left. That way the people who bought the place after would have to clean up after them. Their memory. Then she got a place in this area, which is why he moved here. His brother never wanted to move here. He got married quickly and now he's divorced. Their mother had another child who doesn't even know about how she bought drugs from a kid in the neighborhood at one time. Evan's happy though, because he's met great people here.

Great people might be everywhere. Anywhere. Nowhere. This isn't the place.

Turns out that Lena's still at her sister's or something and, at first, you wonder if there's trouble between them. Maybe the talk he wants to have isn't bad like you thought. Maybe Evan wants to admit to you that he loves you (you have not said this to each other yet even though you've thought it. You write his name in different fonts and sizes so it fills up pages in your English notebook).

Maybe he wants to ask you to be in a real relationship. You hope all of her pictures have been taken off the wall.

You get to his house. He smiles as he opens the door and invites you in. Immediately asks if you want some coffee or hot chocolate or something, and before you answer, you see their wedding picture still hanging above the front room TV.

You could scream.

You tell him no.

He gestures to the couch. You consider ignoring it and walking straight into the bedroom. You think about it, then you do it. You walk past him, into the hallway, and he calls after you, but you disregard it.

"Hey, where are you going?"

You lay on the bed. You stare at the ceiling. No pictures up there.

"What's going on?" He asks immediately upon entering the room.

You don't answer. You're thinking about Sergio from geography class and what he'd look like naked. You're not interested in him, never crushed on him, but it's interesting to think about. You imagine him looking like a beanstalk when naked, although in reality you'll never know.

If Roman was here and asked if you wanted coke, you'd say yes. You want some.

Evan sits next to you at first. Then he lays down too.

"How was school?" He asks, staring at the same ceiling as you.

Truthfully, you skipped almost immediately, after second hour. Jessica stopped by your locker to tell you she'd be staying with her dad sometime soon after stealing some of her mother's jewelry. She didn't know if she'd still go to this school and it made you a little sad. So when she told you she was going to skip, you decided ditching class sounded better anyway. The bell rang. You two left out of a side door with no alarm because no one pays attention to the side doors. You walked around the front and ran across the main road, not even looking for cars. You ran through backyards, hopped fences, grass stains and mud stains from falling. Laughing. You ended up deep in a neighborhood with a park where you both sat on children's swings. Moved gently. Not saying anything.

You tell Evan, "Good. I learned a lot."

He rolls onto his side so he faces you. You stay looking at the ceiling. He hasn't started the conversation yet, not really, but you start crying anyway. He says don't cry. You cry. Little tears, not big. But tears. Tears are tears, you think.

Evan says you must know, and you do.

In a room that you feel like you know everything about, but know so little of. With a man who reminds you that you're sixteen. You'll be seventeen next month. Everything changes. People won't be the same. Never. You are not the same.

Evan's talking to you, and you know what he's saying even without him saying it, without you hearing it. You aren't sure of the words, but his hands are wrapped around yours in a way that makes this clear. You still stare at the ceiling. Tears streak your cheeks. The fabric that your head lies on is growing damp. Evan wipes them away with a finger. One finger is not enough. He tries to wipe again and you push him away.

He says something about how this probably isn't best for you. Something about how you're wonderful blah blah blah he's glad he blah blah met blah blah blah you.

You think about tearing the notebook pages out.

He wants you to know this isn't about you.

How couldn't it be?

It's not your fault.

You think about lighting pictures with him on fire. Then you remember you don't have pictures with him. So you think about setting his pictures on fire. With Lena. All of them. If they're all gone, it's like they never existed.

"Really, I'm glad you stole that cup from the game."

You think about Roman. You haven't seen her in a while. You wonder where she's at.

"This doesn't have to be goodbye. Just… not as often. You still have my number."

He doesn't seem to care that you aren't speaking.

You almost choke. You want to choke.

"So this is it?" You ask.

Clearly frustrated, Evan says no. You think you hear him say, didn't you just hear me? Something about: doesn't need to be goodbye, doesn't need, doesn't, isn't.

You think you hear him say look, get up, or something. He's trying to pull you. You're weighted like an anchor. Not moving. Ceiling.

He invites you to watch American Idol or some kind of karaoke show in the other room. You think about the time that you first met Roman at the gas station, where she asked you what you'd sing at karaoke night. You told her nothing. Nothing. You don't sing.

You think about Roman at a karaoke night, standing on stage in a spotlight. A tank top. Her belly button ring glittering. Her hair down. Not brushed. Her mouth a perfect O. You haven't talked to her in like a week. Evan's somewhere to your side still trying to pull you off the bed.

You think about that karaoke night that Roman never took you to like she promised, and even though you said you don't sing, made up that you'd sing "Smells Like Teen Spirit," you've got the answer now.

You'd sing "I Want It That Way."

Your mother's first boyfriend ended up fucked and in prison. You've heard this story in snippets. Never whole.

Sometime after she met your father, she went down to Mississippi to visit the other guy. You don't know if that was before or after he was arrested, or if it was before or after your father. She met the guy at a friend's pool party, she spent a few months flirting with him, then sleeping with him, then she was too tired to keep it up. She was never devastated when it ended. But then she visited him years later because the things we have now are never enough, you guess. You're not even sure she told your father until she returned. You know very little about this you realize. You also know very little about your mother.

This memory reminds you that you're sure that stories are just that: stories. And it can be assumed that anyone telling a story is an unreliable narrator.

At this point, Evan practically rolls you off the bed. He's done with your shit. You stand. Wobbly knees. Leave his room. Lena's room. Their room. Was your two's room at times. Things change. Always changing. Evan's changing. You met him, he's gone, you're gone. Gone gone gone.

You walk to the front door. Put on your shoes. Evan's behind you. His hand on your shoulder. He leans in to kiss you. First your wet face, messy with snot, then your lips, equally, if not more so, messy with snot. You let him.

He asks or tells you, you aren't sure, to call him when you get home. Let him know you made it safe. You nod your head.

You wipe some snot off your nose and turn so you're facing him.

Evan squares his shoulders and hips. He looks at you with his lips tight, with the skin around his mouth stiff. He steps past you, his left hand not resting on your lower back like usual, and he opens the door. You look outside at the neighbor on an evening walk who is passing the house and you keep staring. Even after the old man is gone.

Evan waits there. He waits in silence, doesn't tell you to leave, but you both know what's inevitable.

Jessica got a tattoo of a heart behind her ear (and also hadn't moved like she was supposed to).

You told her that you knew you and Evan would probably be "over" soon.

"That can't be true. You two are in love."

You didn't tell her that she's wrong.

"What are you going to do?"

Huh?

"To win him back."

The thought hadn't crossed your mind.

The two of you were sitting on the curb outside a party store. Jessica held a pack of Newports because she started smoking last week. She told you she met a boy who reminds her of her father. She likes him so much she let him take photos of her in her bra and underwear. She's not in love yet, but thinks when he fucks her, she will be. That's why she doesn't think you should give up on Evan.

You asked her if her boyfriend is married.

She told you he's not her boyfriend. He's also only nineteen, she met him at a coworker's apartment, so he's probably not married. Then she said, "You could give him what he wants."

And you think, that's how it always goes.

Jessica thinks this is a game, like Evan is a prize, when she says win him back, but she doesn't understand what you understand.

You lean in to hug him. He raises his hand and with the rough flesh of his thumb, wipes some more snot off your face. You feel bare. He tells you you're looking a little red.

You don't say anything.

You hold on a little too long though and eventually he has to remove your arms from his body.

You walk out the door.

Evan locks up behind you. He says there's no turning back. Blah blah blah call him blah when you blah blah get home blah. You want him to stop repeating himself. He says you shouldn't be a stranger, but you both know that's what will happen, because it has to.

You're walking away.

You start humming the song "I Want It That Way," trying to decide how it feels in your throat. Something about the song is strange, so you sing it louder, trying to figure it out.

Then you realize this song played at the party, where you lost Roman and met Evan. Now you've lost Evan.

"What are you singing?" he asks.

"A song." You stop singing to answer him.

"I didn't know you sing."

You didn't either.

Evan steps closer. He doesn't say he'll miss you, but he doesn't have to.

You decide Jessica is right. This must be love. Love shouldn't be too eager though. Something's got to be too eager, but it can't be love – or you.

You give Evan another hug without looking at him.

Evan's nose is against your scalp and he breathes in your scent. You haven't washed it in days so it's not the usual coconut smell that you think makes you more exotic.

"You know I'm not trying to hurt you. Right?" Evan takes your chin in his fingers and tilts your head up toward him. You don't stop him. You say, "I know."

He tries to kiss your lips but this time you turn away. His fingers get caught in your unbrushed hair. He pulls kind of hard and, accident or not, you let him. He makes some sort of pathetic noise. It doesn't matter.

You know you should leave. You also know you'll be back again. Without permission, he pulls kind of hard. He doesn't let go. You think, men should just do everyone a favor and disappear. Still, you breathe like you like it anyway.

This is how you give him what he wants.

Robert, the guy who likes Kelly green and doesn't make passes at women, uses his military money to buy cocaine. You are going to the bathroom in the party apartment when you learn this. You learn this because the powder is cut in lines on the bathroom sink. You still haven't met Robert.

"You saw nothing," Roman laughs, curled up next to two other women on the loveseat when you come back to the living room. One of them smokes a cigarette. She's finished. She burns it out right in the cushion of the sofa where you notice dozens of other similar freckles.

The other woman without a cigarette pushes herself up and stumbles down the hall. You hear the bathroom door shut. You imagine a sugared nose.

Roman asks if you touched it.

You ask where Robert is.

Roman wipes her finger against the ashes left on the couch and presses it to her lips. She licks it.

Robert walks in the front door. He waves to you all and carries a brown McDonald's bag. He doesn't say hi to you, but not in a mean way.

You watch him walk into the small kitchen beside you and empty the bag. There are no burgers. It's a few more plastic pouches of coke.

Later you're sitting between Roman and the woman with the cigarette, and the other woman sits on Roman's lap, her legs spread across you. You are trapped. She can't stop talking. She talks about painting her nails, soccer dad bumper stickers, and antennas on the backs of cars. Robert has turned this into a drinking game. He says everyone has to take a drink whenever the woman interrupts to talk. She doesn't even know why you're all getting drunk. What's her name?

Robert sits on the floor in front of you. He touches your knee that's still sticking out from beneath the woman's legs. He asks if you want the best twenty minutes of your life and why not.

She says owls say who and none of you know what she's talking about but you laugh and take a drink. No one says where the guy who owns this apartment is. Does he even live here. Robert waves you down the hall. Says have you ever tried this before. You shake your head no. You tell him you want to though. He smiles. In the bathroom he tells you step by step how. You lean over the sink and he holds back your hair for you. You miss at first. He doesn't tell you to switch nostrils. Your nose bleeds. You have blood and powder all over the sink and he still smiles. You think you get enough up there, how do you know, but you start telling Robert he's really cute. You're sure he blushes. He looks nice in blush. You grab his hand, you take it, feels like firm, you're not sure what he says. Don't remember, but you feel like kissing him sloppy. You start telling him about an artist you like, but you don't know the name. Somewhere in France. Dead you think. Must be dead. An angel in the water. Also dead. Glowing. She looks so beautiful it's like she's sleeping. You know she's an angel because of her halo. Wrists tied. A painting. So beautiful.

You find yourself buried in Roman's shoulder when everyone else is asleep because you can't stop the knocking on your heart, like someone wants in. She says shh and rubs the back of your neck but you just want everything to stop like just don't breathe. But how don't you. You feel your fingers, too tiny, you feel your lips, so dry. You want to bang your head against her collarbone but she won't let you and you need more more more. Like how did you ever love anyone in this room that much but you don't even know where the others went you're just in Roman's arms trying not to explode.

Jessica's friend Katie brought her razor to school. It was small and shiny and sharp. At the start of English class, she showed it to you and said, "You can cut me if you really want." You didn't want to. The thought had never crossed your mind. She put the razor on her lap. It stayed in your view. You couldn't help but stare at it. You focused on the weapon long enough, until you could imagine yourself wielding it, as the one conducting the pain. Teacher had five questions on the board, about the story you were supposed to read last night. You didn't answer them. The only one you noticed was the last one that said, "How does the author depict the gradual breakdown of civilization? What symbols does he use to represent this savagery?"

No, you don't want a ride. You look Evan in his eyes, spaced a little too evenly apart, and excuse yourself to the bathroom. You hear him protest behind you, think he reaches his hand out, weakly calling after you, but you shut his bedroom door as you leave.

You notice more pictures of Evan and Lena hanging in their hallway.

Lena in a 50s-style polka dot bathing suit, hanging on Evan's semi-muscled arm and whispering through a lemon-slice grin next to a black cross earring in his ear. His scar over his heart.

Evan in a Christmas-striped sweater, his arms wrapped warmly around Lena who's on the ground in front of him, sitting against his legs. Her hair is curly. His hair is gelled down in a James Dean way.

Lena's face underneath her hands like she's crying, in a cherry sundress. Evan in blue jeans, on one knee. Holding a small box in his hands.

You take this picture down, enter the bathroom, and practically scream.

You vacuumed a ladybug one time. Saw it sitting on the wall, it was obvious – a red dot against an off-white – and it made you angry. Disgusted. Invaded. You grabbed the vacuum and extension, tightening the two together, and caught the bug under the hose. Hard against the wall, you turned the vacuum on and it immediately started storming. A rush as it tried to suck in what it could. Only a few seconds went by before you turned off the machine. You hadn't been able to see what it did to the bug, but you knew it had been removed. You lifted the tube and you were right. Bye-bye, ladybug. It doesn't take much at all to destroy something. Make it like it was never there at all.

Evan's knocking on the bathroom door.

"Is everything okay in there? I hear screaming."

"Everything's fine. I don't know what you're talking about."

You're opening each bathroom drawer right now and going through them. Deodorant in different scents: old spice and almond. Tweezers shaped like a woman's silhouette. Hair scrunchies that look like they're from the eighties. An old plastic razor that should be thrown out – so you do it for them. You lift the small garbage can's lid with your foot and drop the razor into the trash. Still looking through drawers: a makeup bag with two tubes of Cover Girl lipstick and a new bottle of mascara. Three folded washcloths. An almost-empty bottle of Zoloft.

"Open up."

"No."

"I'll get the key," he says and, of course, you think. There is a key.

"I'm going pee," you say, turning on the sink to its lowest setting so it sounds like something's dribbling.

"Open up when you're done."

"Sure," you yell.

A package of new toothbrushes, unopened. Another bottle of Zoloft. Lotion for hands. Lotion for face. Travel-sized bottles of toothpaste. The sketch of what looks to be a possible tattoo. It's a dreamcatcher. You're not sure who it's meant for, Evan or Lena. You put the almost-empty bottle of Zoloft in your pocket.

"Are you done yet?" Evan's still outside the door. His voice comes from the floor. He must be lying down, looking, talking, underneath the crack.

"It's a long piss."

"I don't believe you."

You shrug. You realize he can't see your movement.

You walk over to the tiny window next to the shower. Using the lever, you open it and hope it doesn't squeak. It does.

"What's happening?"

Uhh. "You should get a new toilet."

You throw the picture of Evan and Lena outside, into a bush that's on the side of the house.

The doorknob starts to rattle like Evan's unlocking it. He's working on fitting the key in, so you hurry with the window. Shut the drawer. Lather up your hands and start washing. Water rushing down.

"I'm washing my hands, Evan. I'll be out in a second."

You can't figure out why he's being so needy right now.

There was a time you did the same thing, tried breaking into a bathroom. Kia locked herself in, but that time she'd kept the key. Smart girl. She had the house phone hostage and told you to get lost. Didn't even pretend like she was going pee.

Her boyfriend Daren broke up with her an hour before. This was after she broke up with him the previous day. Neither one of them could, or would, commit to each other. You're sure they just liked the idea of each other. Reality is a different story.

She'd been hanging out with Daren and Kyle and June. Kyle and June were dating, on good terms, and kissing one another in the basement when Daren begged Kia to just talk to him. Kia hid in different spots around Kyle's house. Daren kept finding her. Then she left, and he kept calling her. She knew if she answered, they'd get back together. Then he'd break up with her next week. Even at, like, fourteen, she knew they would be a cycle.

So the phone kept going off, which you couldn't get to, and Kia sat somewhere on the bathroom floor and she didn't want to talk to anybody, not even you, because it meant facing her inability to be with anyone. People would ask frequently if she was going to get back together with Daren. People included you. But what does together mean? Just sitting next to one another? Being comfortable? How does it compare to putting two books in a box together?

Kia did not let you in the bathroom. She stopped answering you. She put the phone under a pile of towels. Didn't stop screaming until eventually Daren gave up calling.

He ended up asking her to the Spring Fling later that month. She said yes. You asked her why she was going with

Daren, were they back together or something, and she told you to shut up.

"What do you want?" You open the door to Evan standing nearly a foot taller than you, looking down at you through some hair hanging in front of his eyes.

Without saying anything, the man pulls you against his chest with a force and kisses your lips.

"What do you want?" You gasp.

"You."

You roll your eyes. His hands feel calloused where he holds your upper arms. You look past him, down the hallway, and notice the empty nail where the photo is missing. He doesn't notice, or at least hasn't mentioned it.

"It's almost eight," he says. Reminding you that you're late for school.

"I know. I'm on my way out."

"All right."

"That's why I'm in the bathroom." You grab his toothbrush from the sink, don't ask if it's okay you use it, and cover it in toothpaste. You wonder if Lena's used his toothbrush like this before.

He says, "I've got new toothbrushes in the drawer," but you wave your hand at him. Uh-uh. Toothbrush in your mouth. Shake your head. You're fine.

He leaves you alone to finish cleaning yourself.

You've only known him a few months, but you think about it. About how that's all it takes to get lost. Actually, just a few hours is all it takes to get lost.

"Remember when you took my cup?"

"Yeah, and then you dropped a ping pong ball in it."

"It's like I was flirting with you or something."

Laugh, laugh, laugh.

"I had no idea."

"I'm not sure if I wanted you to."

Some things never change.

This conversation happened last night, where you reimagined how you two met. How you two got together. Memories will never be truthful.

You think of Roman, leaning against your car, telling you she just got out of prison. No. She told you you'd sing at karaoke. She told you about prison the next time you saw each other. Or after she said you'd sing. She called you to ask for a lift to the convenience store and, if you recall, you had to pick up tampons from there anyway, so you told her yes. Tampons, or pads, or makeup wipes. It's hard to remember. Nothing's real, and no one would know which was the lie if you and Roman both told different ways you met each other. No one would know if they were both lies.

You pick through the drawer again, find the makeup bag, pull out the red lipstick. The tube says its name: "Move Over, On Fire." You wonder if that's a name or a warning. What if we all had warnings printed on the bottom of us?

Pulling off the cap, you swipe Lena's makeup across your lips in a few different directions. Pucker up. Check yourself out in the mirror. Your lips look new.

You put the lipstick in your pocket. A souvenir you will wear again and again. You will wear it to a party where you will be too eager to stain some man's throat. You will wear it to the mall while you browse Cosmopolitan magazines without buying them. You will wear it to bed when you fall asleep with your makeup on. In doing so, you will remind men of their wives. No, you will remind them of a girl configuring herself while the rest of the world cheers. Those might be the same thing.

Your lips look unrecognizable in the mirror. Then you figure it out. Why your lips look so different. Suddenly you look like all the women he's loved before.

You don't believe he'll even look at these lips and recognize the difference. You might not anymore either.

Last week Evan told you that he drove past the local crematory and could smell the bodies sizzling. He knew it was bodies he smelt. It was like someone in the neighborhood was barbecuing. Like they were grilling steaks. He stopped his car because he said they smelled so good. Then he couldn't stop thinking about it.

That's the thing that stuck with him. The fact that he'd rather remember that the burning bodies smelled so delicious than the idea that the people inside were watching the bodies burn.

Evan tries asking if you're done again.

You want to tell him move over. You tell him you're leaving instead. You smell gasoline as you walk past him.

You get to the front porch and an olive-green car pulls up like it belongs there because it does. A woman climbs out. You are still standing on the porch, dumb, like you don't have legs.

The woman is expectedly nondescript. Still, you know exactly who she is. You recognize her. You are still convinced you wouldn't though if you met her anywhere else. She's that kind of woman.

You hate to think she's some kind of beautiful.

You take small steps down the stairs, polite. She's holding a paper bag full of something tight against her chest. You can't see inside. You don't really want to see inside.

You notice the ring on her finger even though you're not close enough to see its beauty or worth. You look at her face, her body, and wonder what made her choose this life. Get this life.

You stop. You don't even say hi, but you tell her you hate her ring. You say, "It's not even real."

Roman told you that the one time when you were looking at a pretty diamond dream. Things aren't real. Reality is never the same. Always changing.

Lena's mouth opens. She asks who you think you are. Who you are. Who thinks. Bitch.

Maybe you're not supposed to say something like what you did.

What is truth. Maybe that's why people don't like it. Because who knows.

Evan told you one time that Lena is self-conscious about her lips. You figure that's mostly why she wears lipstick. She changes their color, their shape. She wants more than anything to change their appearance, so no one else knows how utterly repulsive they are.

She's saying something. "You can leave," maybe.

You scrunch your eyes up and look at her mouth. They'd look kind of like a heart if they weren't so thin. You place your finger to your own lips, to draw attention to them. Yours are full and kind of round. You've decided yours are nice. They are nicer than hers, anyway. You smear the lipstick a little.

You hear the storm door open and shut behind you. Evan's weight on the front porch.

"What are you doing?" he says.

You are not sure which one of you he is talking to, although it's probably you. You don't answer. Lena can. Might be the same thing.

"Evan," she says. Evan. She looks like some kind of performance art, with her manufactured lips and small diamond earrings.

"Answer me," he says, only looking at you. He ignores Lena.

You look back at him. Like you are trying to figure something out. Maybe you both are. This doesn't really matter.

"Stop being a cunt," you hear him finally say. Like he's been waiting this whole time to say it.

You want to know what it must be like to have enough women you think are yours that you can call them that and not be concerned. You would like to know what it must be like to have enough of anything for that matter.

You imagine him coming up to you and gripping the back of your head. Your hair knotted around his fingers. His shadow, crestfallen against your body. He is some sort of recital next to his wife. She says nothing.

"I'm leaving."
"Is that what you're doing?"

Knot gets tighter.
Head pulled back.

"Absolutely."
"What is that you're saying?"
A bird chirps.

"Stop." Your eyes are closed.
Words escape your lips.

Lena might have dropped her bag. Grabbed his arm. You see four tubes of lipstick on the ground.

He says, "But you're not."
His hands move. Around your neck now. You grab his wrists. Feel his pulse.

He holds you like he means it.
This is all you want. Right here. With Lena watching.

Then you open your eyes to look into his. Realize he's still a foot away from you.

You like the attention though. Even if it's not real. You wish what you imagined was true.

He says, "Look, don't talk to Lena like that."
Like things are normal or something.
"Sure."
But what did you even say? Rings aren't real. Love is something else.

The three of you are still in front of his house, on public display.

You move forward. Push against his chest. You think you say, "I don't even want you." You can't be sure because that's not true.
Evan laughs at you. Like he knows you're a liar.
You realize Lena's been watching you this whole time. She probably thinks she's prettier than you.
You realize that your smeared lipstick probably looks like blood.

You were twelve the first time it happened, in a tie-dye bathing suit from the sale rack of the department store, and in your neighbor's inflatable swimming pool. Dennis was thirteen and useless. You asked him to synchronize swim with you, but he couldn't follow your lead even if his life depended on it. You told him look, just kick your right leg. He didn't know left from right. Then you spun in a circle. That must be easy for him to do, but he made gagging noises. Shouted out, "Gross!" He said, "What is wrong? Are you dying?"

You looked down. A violent eruption circled you. It was red, and it was unclear from where it was coming, but you thought Dennis was right. Maybe you were dying.

You started crying, jumped out of the water and jogged home, expecting to smash into the sidewalk and bleed out, like road kill blistered on the street.

You made it inside your house and shouted for your mother.

I'm dying, you yelled. I won't survive.

Your blood dripped down your child-thighs.

When she walked in the front room a few minutes later she tossed you a cheap pad with no explanation and went back to bed.

The next day you told Kia she was lucky you were still alive, although you weren't sure how with how much blood you were still losing. You wouldn't stop.

"My mom says we all do that."

"We who?"

"Women."

"Why?"

It needs to happen so one day you can get pregnant.

But what if you don't want to get pregnant?

"Well, think of your future husband. What if he wants you to?"

You'd rather be dying.

You pull out your keys. It's been like five or ten minutes or something and you still haven't made it to your car. Closer, but not enough. Here. Stuck here. Lena somewhere there. Evan and his force. She's stopped reacting. Evan says it's time to go home now. Lena's a statue. Something to look at, but only because someone says it's important. She's the last person you want to imagine Evan alone with. You've got your keys between two fingers. You turn to Lena's car behind you. Drag your key across her driver's side door.

You scream.

You think Lena screams.

Evan doesn't. He's holding your arm – the space just above your elbow – you don't let him stay there. Slip yourself out. Your mother taught you how to twist your arm to release a grab when you were a child. She saw it on a women's defense lesson on a news segment once.

Lena reaches for you. You drag. Walk ten feet. Evan's car. Right there. Scratch and drag.

Evan's got your shoulders. He won't stop you. One wretched line. At a time. Then another.

You are not caught off guard. By the snot on your lips. The noise in your throat. The storm in your heart. You know the wreckage that women can cause.

You feel two people pulling you. You think a stranger walks past uncertainly.

You're almost done.

Lena has to know what you're feeling. You don't trust her. This is a show. Is this why he stays with her?

You finish. You're proud. Your graffiti says *Nothing's real.*

Evan had told you that the question game was a scientific study. That it was supposed to make you fall in love. He asked you questions. You asked him questions. He wants to learn to skateboard. He said you were authentic. You eventually had sex. He never pulled your hair. You didn't fall in love. Even science can't get it right.

You drop down on the driveway that has wild dandelions spreading in the cracks. You think about Roman. Wonder where she is. What problems of her own she's caught up in.

There's chaos behind you. All around you. Two people who won't touch you now. Police car sirens in the distance.

Eye level with your humiliating autograph, you lean toward it. It's perfect. You do not feel like what you did or what you're about to do is wrong. You feel satisfied. With Lena's red lipstick on, you press your lips against the steel and leave a big, sloppy kiss.

You wonder if she recognizes it.

NOTES

Songs and their musical artists referenced include:

"Hungry Like the Wolf" by Duran Duran
"Smells Like Teen Spirit" by Nirvana
"This Is How We Do It" by Montell Jordan
"U Can't Touch This" by MC Hammer
"Where Is My Mind?" by Pixies
"It's Not Over" by Daughtry
"I Want It That Way" by Backstreet Boys

The painting referred to on page 183 is *The Young Martyr / La Jeune Martyre*, an oil painting by the painter Paul Delaroche.

Arthur Aron developed thirty-six questions for his research on ways to forge interpersonal closeness. The study that is referred to, and the similar questions that are used in this book, starting on page 147, is discussed in the article "The Experimental Generation of Interpersonal Closeness: A Procedure and Some Preliminary Findings" (1997) by Arthur Aron, Edward Melinat, Elaine N. Aron, Robert Darrin Vallone, and Renee J. Bator.

VISIT

www.RaisingWomen.weebly.com

TO DOWNLOAD THE RAISING WOMEN BOOK CLUB KIT

ACKNOWLEDGMENTS

There are so many people who helped make this book a reality, and for that I'm so extremely grateful.

From the bottom of my heart, thank you Xavier Iriarte, Elisabeth "Em" Marcus, and Melissa Marguerite for your repeated reads and thorough help on this piece. There is no way it would be where it is without your support (and, again, many reads).

For additional close readings that allowed this story to be even better than I thought, I credit Kaitlyn Armstrong, B. Benford, Rae Harrison, Paul Lacoursiere, Ilze Lucero, Kim McNulty, and Ivy. I appreciate you volunteering your time more than you know.

The women-led team who made this book come to life is truly the best. Lindee Robinson provided the perfect photos, marketing materials, and brainstorming, on top of always being my biggest cheerleader. Najla Qamber and Nada Qamber worked hard with me to make the perfect cover and a beautiful interior. All of these ladies are so positive and I'm grateful they were excited to be on my team.

Thanks to Annie Gilson, Peter Markus, and the English and Creative Writing department at Oakland University for their constant support. I will never regret my two degrees from here.

To my readers, I appreciate you more than you know. My writing is constantly growing so I can write stories that speak to you. If you picked up this book and read it, know that it means the world to me.

To all the women whose books have found a home on my shelves (like Selah Saterstrom, Elizabeth Ellen, Miranda July, and many others) and have inspired me to write about women, thank you. Thanks also goes to Miles Marie and Melissa Marguerite for recommending these incredible authors who inspired this book. You can ask these ladies: I used to write solely from the points of view of men. Maybe it's because, at that time, that's all I was reading.

Thank you to Zak, my husband, for understanding when I decided it was time for another degree, and for encouraging me when I come up with big ideas.

Finally, my greatest gratitude goes out to all the girls I grew up with. This one's for you.

ABOUT THE AUTHOR

Award-winning writer and educator Shannon Waite writes stories about norms, characters who break norms, and society's wounds. They're always contemporary, often transgressive. Her debut novel, *Raising Women*, is an interactive novel in which readers make self-destructive decisions that explore the wild that is growing up girl.

Her short fiction has been published in *Pank*, *Hobart*, and elsewhere. She has two bachelor's degrees in English and Creative Writing from Oakland University and an MA in Teaching and Curriculum from Michigan State University. Shannon teaches English and Creative Writing in Detroit, Michigan where she lives with her husband, cat, and hamster.

Visit her online at: www.shannonwaiteauthor.com
Facebook.com/shannonwaiteauthor
Instagram: @shannonwaiteauthor

If you enjoyed

RAISING WOMEN

look out for

THE WOMEN
A Raising Women Expansion Pack

Raising Women is an interactive novel that explores the themes of womanhood and reality through the second person point of view where readers get to choose what happens in the story. Shannon Waite's upcoming collection is titled *The Women*. Think of *The Women* as an expansion pack – an addition to an existing role-playing game that offers new characters, settings, and extended storylines.

The Women will be a collection of short stories about the women in *Raising Women*. These stories will explore events mentioned in *Raising Women*, as well as new character experiences that were not previously mentioned. This book gives readers the opportunity to learn more about the characters they loved in the previous book and explore more themes surrounding womanhood, reality, and identity.

ROMAN

My jeans were unzipped when the cop pulled me over, but it was a happy mistake.

Late at night, traffic lights sprinting in my peripherals. I saw his siren first, I mean heard it, saw his flashers. I knew there'd be trouble.

My pants were already unzipped. That was an accident. I didn't do it for him.

But because my zipper was down, the first thing he didn't catch was me texting on my phone. The second thing he didn't catch was the cocaine under my back seat.

He was tall enough, sandpaper scruff along his jaw, and a triangular nose. His badge was perfect-straight.

"Miss."

He tried to look me in the eyes.

"Yes? …I'm sorry."

Still trying to look me in the eyes. My hands were on my waistline.

"Miss" and then, "I shouldn't be doing this" sitting in my passenger seat. He put his hands on my panties.

I didn't think anything of it, didn't tell him to stop, it's not my job to tell him to stop. Afterall, we make bad decisions around here. So I let him. Told him it's okay. I undressed myself like a carnival show, some kind of celebration. He watched.

It didn't take long. We were on the side of the expressway, his flashers still flashing, headlights whizzing by. My phone buzzing under his heavy breathing, sister asking where the coke's at. I'd get back to her later. The cop kissed me goodbye. He told me no ticket this time. I almost spit.

I zipped my pants up. The New York Times said unbuttoned jeans are a fashion statement now-a-days but I was only full from dinner. I started the ignition, turned the lefthand blinker on to let everyone know I was leaving the shoulder, rejoined traffic, and drove off without a ticket. Because a man won't even really look. If he'd bothered, he'd have found what he was actually looking for.

RAISING WOMEN

Games

ROMAN'S MASH

Traditionally, MASH is a fortune telling game where players create categories and then predict their future in those categories. With a random number, you count down each item until you reach the item that falls on that number. Cross off that option. Repeat, crossing off each item that falls on that number until one result is left in each category.

PET	JOB
Black Labrador	Who knows
Squirrel	Astronaut
Cat corpse	Nurse
Goldfish	Janitor
CAR	**KIDS**
Cadillac	One
No car	Three
Mom mini-van	Forty
Box car	Abort them

(Are the items you picked the things that end up happening in the book?)

Answers are on the back of this page.

Answers
Cat corpse, who knows, no car, abort them

ROMAN'S NEVER HAVE I EVER

In the group game Never Have I Ever, everyone stands in a circle. Each person shares something he or she has never done. **If anyone in the group has done that thing, they take a drink.**

As the people in the group list off the things they've never done, **how many things has Roman done? (How many drinks does she take?)**

Gone to prison
Caught best friend railing younger sister
Stolen a pair of combat boots
Stolen wine from a church
Gotten you to try coke
Wanted children
Gotten pregnant
Shown others her list of prettiest girls
Got arrested at a house party

Total drinks: _______

Answers are on the back of this page

Answers

Total drinks: 4

Roman has gone to prison, caught best friend railing younger sister, stolen wine from a church, and gotten pregnant

YOUR NEVER HAVE I EVER

In the group game Never Have I Ever, everyone stands in a circle. Each person shares something he or she has never done. **If anyone in the group has done that thing, they take a drink.**

As the people in the group list off the things they've never done, **how many things have you done? (How many drinks do you take?)**

Snorted coke off a bathroom counter
Gotten pregnant
Hooked up with a man at least ten years older
Had a belly button ring
Gotten drunk alone
Drawn a dick on a telephone pole
Took a cup of alcohol from a beer pong table
Strip for three boys at a party

Total drinks: _______

Answers are on the back of this page

YOUR TWO TRUTHS AND A LIE

In the game Two Truths and a Lie, someone lists off two things that are true, and one thing that is not true, about him or herself.

Which is your lie?

> You cut off your own eyelashes
> You burned your pictures with Evan
> You went to the West House bathroom looking for sex

Answers are on the back of this page

Answer
You burned your pictures with Evan

www.ingramcontent.com/pod-product-compliance
Lightning Source LLC
Chambersburg PA
CBHW061526310726
48972CB00008B/2340